JULY 2024 - ISSUE 214

FICTION

NON-FICTION

Neil Clarke: Publisher/Editor-in-Chief
Sean Wallace: Editor
Kate Baker: Non-Fiction Editor/Podcast Director

Clarkesworld Magazine (ISSN: 1937-7843) • Issue 214 • July 2024

Every Hopeless Thing
TIA TASHIRO

Elodie finds a pair of old opera glasses in the empty husk of an abandoned silo. The gleam of the metal catches her flashlight beam and throws it back, and Elodie squats and fishes out the glasses with tentative fingers. The silo is huge and dark around her, so quiet her footsteps echoing sounds like trespass, but the glasses are proof it was once inhabited. Perhaps a family found their way here in the early days of the collapse, huddled up with canned foods and lead blankets in the last place anyone would think to look.

Elodie carefully tucks the opera glasses into an inside pocket of her scavenging pack. She stands and dusts her gloves off on her thick, shielded pants. The gauge on the inside of her soft plastic helmet is reading at acceptable levels of ambient pollution, nothing that would breach her suit; it would alarm if she hit unsafe levels, and she'd hotfoot it back to Skip and let the medical system give her a once-over if it did.

At least the pollution is the only thing she has to worry about. Earth's a dead planet, after all.

When she landed her skipper outside the silo, maneuvering it precisely into a dusty field bereft of all but a few hardy plants still gripping the soil, she was struck by the nakedness of the ground. Elodie knows her history as well as any of the human diaspora, the spacefarers who escaped the fate of their land-bound relatives, and it still stole the breath from her lungs to face the murdered world.

She finds a few empty metal cans, the insides long ago molded into black, but nothing still unopened. That's a disappointment; some geneticists will pay out the airlock for a bit of DNA scrounged from a canned pineapple or orange, convinced they can reverse-engineer fruits that have been lost to the past. Most scavengers don't bother with Earth these days, though. The wreckage of the planet has been thoroughly picked over, and besides, it's hard to find relics when most major cities have been nuked off the map.

That said, Elodie's done her research to locate promising sites for this planetary foray, and she doesn't want anyone else scooping her finds. She's lucky her skipper keeps her secrets. It's not like a corporation scavenger, recording her location and movements in case she finds something a little too rich for her blood. She paid a programmer in a Mars colony to strip the spyware out of it, give it a new and better voice. *Her* skipper is no snitch.

Elodie's stomach growls. Her scavenging pack is still too light on her back, and she's starting to get annoyed. She'd had high hopes for the silo, thought she'd be able to dig out some ancient tech, but parts of it have collapsed, and it's too dangerous for her to go on alone.

Hungry? Skip's tone in her earpiece is light, teasing.

The corner of Elodie's mouth quirks up despite herself. "Spying on me? I thought I was too far from your primaries."

If I can hear your spoken responses, Pilot Elodie, I can keep myself updated on your gastrointestinal status. Primary sensors or no. Skip plays a short snippet of a song they both like, an inside joke from a scavenging stint on a faraway moon: its version of laughter. *Don't starve on my watch, Pilot, I'd never forgive myself. And besides, who'd fly me out of here?*

"Okay, okay." Her encroaching bad mood quelled, Elodie trudges back out into the smoggy deadness of the world and squints as her eyes adjust. Her gauge blips upward as she leaves the silo, no longer shielded from the ultraviolet radiation that cascades down through the slow-healing ozone layer.

Skip's right. She could use a meal, something cool and filling. As the sun beats down on her face shield, she presses a button at her wrist to activate the tiny fans embedded around her head.

Skipper perches on its four spindly legs, ready to fold them back up and take for the skies when Elodie tells it to. A history of dents and scratches mars Skip's surface, though for the most part, Elodie has been able to fix up its exterior—like when she traded a few loads of scavenged debris for a new paint job, or straightened out one of its bent legs with some elbow grease and a few hours of effort. She smiles as she approaches. She likes to think Skip has the bearing of a long-suffering soldier, wounds stitched into faded scars by a gentle hand. Its belly hangs low to the ground, casting a thick shadow where its form blocks out the sun.

Elodie's thinking about a porridge slush mixed up with a few cranberries—a DNA sequence that *did* manage to be saved before the collapse—as she slams her hand against the hatch opener. It slides open with a smooth *whoosh*, and Elodie takes one step forward. That's all the steps she gets before something hits her at the ankles. She goes down hard, suit thumping against the dusty ground and body thumping against the suit. *Pilot Elodie*, Skipper whirs in her ear, its additional sensory functions woken when she opened the door. *Status report?*

Elodie twists, kicking at her assailant—another scavenger dropping a bot to sabotage her, despite her precautions?—and her boot makes contact. The thing lets go, and Elodie scrambles back, reaching for her extendable.

It's not a sabotage bot. It's not a bot at all.

Status report? Skipper says again, this time adding an urgency marker in the corner of Elodie's helmet. *Hostile? Bot? Pilot, requesting response.*

"It's not a bot, Skip," she says, still unable to believe her eyes. "It's a kid."

Several Years Ago

Log Cycle ????.?, Camellian Corporation Skipper Internal Processing
Olfactoreceptor feed: NULL.
Video feed: NULL.
Audio feed:
VOICE1:—hit, shit, shit, please tell me you work—YES. Come on, little guy, get me out of here—okay, okay,please be the right button—
Text output: Manual override engaged. Booting independent life support systems. Thirty seconds until transport self-sufficiency.
VOICE1: *Shit* yes! Come on, little guy, hurry up if you can! We don't have all—
VOICE2 (note: distant): She's stealing *that one?!*
VOICE3 (note: closer): Hey, you! Get out of there!
VOICE1: Sorry, folks, not today—come on, come *on.*
Text output: Life support systems temporarily functional. Recommend diagnostics and repair to critical infrastructure before any attempt at space travel. Lacking starboard propulsion. Lacking water reclamation sheets. Lacking waste collec—
VOICE1: No time for that, bud, we're on the clock.
VOICE2 (note: loud): THAT'S COMPANY PROPERTY, YOU LITTLE—
VOICE1: Let's *go!*
Text output: Manual override accepted. Undocking now.
VOICE1: Woohoo! YES! That's what I'm talking about! Okay, only a little farther to go—

Text output: Navigation systems damaged. Manual navigation required.
VOICE1: That's okay, bud. It can't be *too* hard to fly you. We'll figure it out. Just relax and enjoy the ride, yeah? I'll take it from here.
Text output: Port propulsion activated.
VOICE1 assigned designation: PILOT.

The kid that tackles Elodie is small, really small, and weirdly pale, like the pigment has bleached out of their skin and hair. They have a rock clutched in one hand. But what most worries Elodie is that the kid—the inexplicable human kid—is *not wearing a suit.*

Elodie kicks into gear before she realizes she's made a decision. She grabs for the kid's weird, knitted tunic, scoops the screeching child up with one hand, and tosses them bodily into Skip, urgency boosting her movements. She jumps through the hatch and slams it shut behind her, cutting them off from the pollutants layered across the Earth's surface in a cancerous mass.

"Skip," she says, breathing hard, "how's flush?"

Flushing carcinogenic elements, Skip reports, *stand by.* It's a lot easier to rid a space of pollutants when it's enclosed, controllable. Some spacefarers have proposed cleansing Earth, but they usually get shut down. The planet's a lost cause; it'd cost too much, and all they'd have to show for it would be barren wastes. They'd practically need to terraform it from scratch to get it livable again.

The kid starts yelling something in a language Elodie doesn't speak. "Skip?" she says.

On it. Skip wires up a translation hub in her helmet, and the kid's voice comes through, partially translated as the hub gets to work mapping the unknown dialect. A word here, a phrase there. They're talking about . . . a curse?

"I'm getting the kid to the med system," Elodie says, ignoring the child's rant.

Already prepped, says Skip, reading her mind, and this is why a sentient spacecraft is Elodie's best friend.

The med system has restraints built in, ostensibly for spacefarers who must be kept under control as the system helps work foreign toxins out of their systems. The auto-adjuster cuffs, on their smallest setting, are still almost big enough for the kid to yank out of—but not quite. At first, the kid writhes on the med system table, screeching about curses, but then they quiet and just start sobbing, snot trickling out of their nose. The latter makes Elodie much more uncomfortable.

Skipper's presence buzzes in her ear. It'll be watching the scene just as Elodie does, as the med system assesses the kid's radiation exposure and seeks out any cancerous cells to quash. If they've caught it in time, the system will be able to localize any mutations down to the cellular level, destroying the individual cells with the phalanx of immunonanites currently coursing through the kid's system. If they're too late, if malignance has already settled in, ballooning the kid's cells into unnatural blooms of tumors too big to remove without catastrophic effects . . .

Relax, Pilot, Skipper says to her ear, its cameras picking up the tension in her shoulders. *You've done what you can.*

Elodie doesn't look away from the kid. Their eyes look red, raw. "Skip—can you turn down your internal lights a notch?"

Good idea. It complies, dimming the illumination in the medical bay. The med system reports an immediate slowing of the kid's heartbeat. Without Elodie needing to ask, Skipper keeps dimming until the medbay is lit somewhere between dusk and twilight.

The med system is telling me the scan is complete, Skip says. *They're clean.*

"Oh, thank god," Elodie mutters. She's not a mother and never wants to be, but she *is* a decent human being; she can't imagine hurting a kid. Speaking of which . . . "How's the translation hub?"

Basic communication should be possible. The language appears to be a permutation of an Earth dialect in my systems—basis in Indo-European. The hub has extrapolated based on the child's input.

"Great. Translate for me, will you, Skip?"

Confirmed.

"So, kid," she addresses the child on the table, who has calmed enough to look her way. She wants to just say what she's thinking: *Are you some meteor baron's heir? Did your parents get in the middle of an asteroid miner's turf war and some jerk dumped you on Earth to die?* But these are questions too pointed, too likely to result in a fresh burst of tears. So Elodie just says, "Who did this to you? You can talk in your language. Skip— my friend will translate."

The kid's gaze darts around the medbay, furtive. "You're safe here," Elodie says. "I mean, as much as we can make you. Sorry about the cuffs, you were kind of freaking out. Skip, disengage?"

Sure thing. The restraints around the kid's wrists open, and they yank their arms out from the metal's clutch. They don't try to move from the table—seem to realize there's no point.

"Who did this to you?" Elodie repeats, attempting patience.

"Who did what?" the kid asks, and at first Elodie thinks it's sass until their expression registers. Confusion.

"Dumped you on this planet," Elodie clarifies. *What a cruel fate*, she thinks. *If I hadn't found you when I did . . . you poor thing.* The kid's brow furrows as Skip translates. It repeats itself, but the message doesn't seem to go through. *I don't think they know what a planet is*, Skip chirps in Elodie's ear. "Okay," Elodie says, trying a different phrasing. "Where are you from?" What distant solar system, what deep-space freighter, what generation ship?

The kid says a word and points. Down. Beneath their feet.

They say . . . Undertown, Skip translates. *Or . . . that's the closest analog I can get.*

Undertown. The finger pointing down. The absence of a protective suit.

"Oh my god," Elodie breathes.

The kid is from *Earth*.

Earth's a dead planet. Nobody lives on Earth; the spacefarer scientists all discounted the possibility centuries ago. No one could survive the UV radiation still buffeting the planet's surface, nor the bevy of pollutants permeating the dirt. It was a painful death for the ones who chose to stay, for the ones who had no choice. Elodie grew up giving remembrance to Earth and the many skeletons the planet still carries, once a year. Offering her respect to the original birthplace of the spacefaring race.

Elodie has always been impressed by the resourcefulness of the spacefarers. It's a grudging respect, at times, for those who use their creativity to make life worse for everyone else; an earned respect for the ones who adapt to new systems and envision ways of living Elodie could never imagine.

She had forgotten that the spacefarers' ancestors were human, too. She had forgotten that they could have been pushed to resourcefulness, to do what they must to survive.

The girl—she refers to herself with a feminine pronoun, Skip's translator hub has determined—is calm, now, hands wrapped around a mug of bland broth Skip reconstituted from its stores. She comments that the soup tastes like mutton, and Skip tells her, speaking in its own voice, that it is a synthesized beef/mutton blend. This earns it a small and tentative smile. If Elodie had known all it took to get through the girl's guard was soup, she would've popped a thermos in the kid's hand *before* she had to resort to med system restraints. Live and learn, she supposes.

The girl tells them her name is Rya, and that she lives deep beneath the surface, in a place called Undertown.

"Are there any other towns like yours?" Elodie asks, trying to walk the thin line between finding out more and asking too many questions.

Rya nods, sipping at her soup. "Except they're far away," she says, making a face. "Deepvalley's closest, but it takes a long time to get there." She kicks her legs as she explains to Elodie and Skip what the Undertowners call the Ghost Road—a long, treacherous series of tunnels and caves. "It's haunted," Rya says seriously. "With all the people who died on it. Like my dad."

Elodie winces. Skip whirs a soft, *oh . . .* in her ear. "I'm sorry," she says.

Rya shrugs. "I don't remember enough to miss him. And *you* didn't kill him. He just left to trade mushrooms with Deepvalley and got caught in a rockfall. At least he wasn't cursed." She shivers. "That would've been worse."

"Cursed," Elodie says, eyebrows lifting. "What's this about a curse?"

Rya sucks down the rest of her soup and looks morosely at the empty cup. Elodie asks Skip to reconstitute another serving, aware that Rya is taking advantage.

Rya grins at the filled mug when Elodie hands it over. "The curse," she says matter-of-factly, "is what kills people who come up to the bright places. Kills 'em slow, usually. Once, one of the preachers that comes through every so often? He showed me pictures." Her face takes on that look of morbid interest in the grotesque Elodie recognizes as belonging to some of the children she's crossed paths with. "They get burns and lumps all over their bodies and their lungs turn black and stuff. It's *so* gross."

Elodie frowns. "*You* came up to the surface."

Rya, briefly, looks chastised. "I don't leave the dark," she defends herself. "So it doesn't count. I only like to come up to look at new things, sometimes." Her gaze dips to the mug. "And new people."

"Like me."

"You're different. I was gonna make you fix it," Rya says, grip tightening around the mug. "Make you fix the curse." She looks up. Hesitant; hopeful. "Can you?"

With a few billion credits and a small army, sure, Elodie thinks.

"Maybe," she says.

Rya's guard is down; she smiles. "Can I bring you back with me? To teach us how?"

No, Skip says.

"Yes," Elodie says. "But first—can you tell me more?"

7

• • •

They talk through two more mugs of soup. Elodie begins to understand the bounds of the kid's worldview, the way the oral history of her people has protected them from the worst of the radiation, the pollutants. A curse makes sense, as far as explanations go. No need to pass down an understanding of the dozens, hundreds, thousands of coinciding environmental disasters that rendered the Earth unlivable. Her sense of history isn't *that* good, but she can guess that in the early days, Rya's ancestors—survivors in a different sense than the spacefarers—would have lost much of the knowledge of what awaited them on the surface, even if they hadn't gone underground before the worst of it hit. Most hadn't been scientists, or environmentalists, or nuclear engineers—just people, who were smart or lucky enough to get somewhere safe and made up stories to keep their children from wandering.

Elodie understands. Still, she can't stop herself from feeling sorry for Rya, sorry for the rest of the humans—the Earthlings!—living sad little lives beneath the crust of the ground. For Elodie, a spacefarer down to her double helices, the thought of being trapped in darkness for a whole lifetime is unimaginable.

"You've uploaded the find to your satellite self?" Elodie asks Skip, keeping her voice low. Rya, spent, has fallen asleep in Elodie's bunk, and Elodie doesn't want to wake her.

Yes, Pilot, Skip reports. Elodie's a scavenger; she's meticulous about the data she keeps. A copy of Skip's consciousness piggybacking on an old Earth satellite now carries the (re)discovery of life on the planet, ready to pass on the info in case something happens to Elodie before she can spread the news. *Please tell me,* Skip says, its voice taking on the long-suffering register of an unwilling partner-in-crime, *that you're not going to confront these people alone.*

"I'm not alone," Elodie says brightly. "I have you."

Several Years Ago

Log Cycle ????.?, Camellian Corporation Skipper Internal Processing
Olfactoreceptor feed: NULL.
Video feed: NULL.
Audio feed:
PILOT: ... and after it stopped responding, I worried I'd fried it. What did you just do?

VOICE4: Reconnected a loose wire. Audio input got shifted in transit. Where'd you say you bought it again? Looks like it used to be a good-quality skipper. *Used to* being the key phrase.

PILOT: I, uh, bought it off a friend.

VOICE4: Some friend they are. Look, this thing's unsalvageable. Half the systems are fritzed. The onboard AI's barely functional—I wouldn't be surprised if it spontaneously decided to space you on an off day. I'll take it off your hands for scrap. Got some friends who're good at taking skiffs like these apart.

PILOT: I . . . I don't know.

VOICE4: I'm doing you a favor here. It's worth just enough for you to hitch a ride on a starfreighter, make your way to one of the new stations on the outer rim. Get yourself a job. I know your type—flighty, but you can make something of yourself if you put down roots somewhere. Trust me. This thing's dead weight.

PILOT: I . . . no. I'm sorry. I appreciate the advice, but I'm keeping it.

VOICE4: I'm only making this offer once. You sure?

PILOT: I'm sure.

Elodie bites back a curse as she sucks in her stomach, just barely squeezing through a channel in the rock to push deeper into the caves. Rya scampers ahead of her with apparent ease, moving over the rocks and through the smallest squish-points with an innate sense of balance and proprioception. They've only been descending for ten minutes, and it's already so dark that Elodie has flicked on all four of her helmet lights. Rya doesn't seem bothered by the absence of light. It's like she's half mole.

What most surprises Elodie is not the cumbersome formations of the subterranean path they're following, nor Rya's willingness to introduce Elodie to Undertown, but the gauge on the inside of her helmet. Only a few minutes down into the dark, it dropped precipitously to acceptable levels of exposure, and the deeper they travel, the lower the percentage of pollutants gets. It's astonishing.

Rya pauses at a hole, smaller than any they've yet pushed through. "This is the last one," she says. "Will you fit?"

Elodie examines the hole, her lights flashing along its jagged edges. She can tell just by looking that it'll be a tight squeeze. She'll make it, she thinks—but not with her helmet on.

Elodie, Skip says, a warning.

"The gauge says it's safe," she murmurs. "I have to get down there. I have to offer them a way out."

You're too stubborn for your own good.

"Stop worrying, Mother Hen." Strangely enough, it's Skip's protest that gives Elodie the boost she needs. She disengages her helmet, pulse jumping as she hears the hiss of the air inside her suit merging with the world around her. As she lifts the helmet off, she gets her first whiff of Undertown—pungent, musky, damp—and immediately indulges in a coughing fit.

Rya asks something from beyond the hole, and Elodie scrambles to detach the earpiece connecting her to Skip from the inside of her helmet. She hooks it onto her ear. *She asked if you're okay*, Skip translates, testy. It's miffed she forgot it in the helmet, she can tell.

"I'm fine," Elodie says gruffly. "Come on. It's time to make some introductions.

Several Years Ago

Log Cycle ????.?, Camellian Corporation Skipper Internal Processing Olfactoreceptor feed: NULL.
Video feed:
Two spacefarers are visible to my cameras. One (dark brown skin, shaved head, tall, focused) is rummaging in my processing core. The other (brown skin, short hair, slightly taller, curious) holds a flashlight to illuminate my internal systems.
Audio feed:
PILOT (note: audio syncs with lip movements of spacefarer with the flashlight; facial features added to PILOT designation): Did you get it?
VOICE5: It's a helluva system. Must have been gorgeous in its prime—mostly a surface lander, but it was modified for a couple of guns, probably for defense. Looks like they took the armaments off it when it was damaged.
PILOT: And you got the GPS?
VOICE5: It was busted anyway, but yeah. If there were any ghost signals still drifting out, I squashed 'em. Looks like the typical company loyalty package was pretty fried, too, but just in case, I'll wipe that clean for free. And I think I just got the cameras working. Give it a wave.
Pilot turns to my [Skipper's] nearest camera and waves. Pilot has a round face and dimples when she smiles. The corners of her eyes crinkle when she looks around the insides of me. She wears loose clothing, not the stiff zipped-up uniforms of the officers I am accustomed to hosting.
VOICE5 spacefarer frowns at my processing core.

VOICE5: Oof. This is a bit more complicated than I was expecting. There's a bug in here, company spyware, you know the type. Record and transmit. These skippers are all snitches. Gonna have to up my fee if you want that scrubbed, on top of all the other junk in here.

Pilot's expression wrinkles into concern. She still faces away from the VOICE5 spacefarer, but I can see her fingers brush against the thin sigil scribed on the inside of her wrist—a temporary financial services access code. I understand.

Text output: Current state is largely nonfunctional.

VOICE5: Oh, hey—

Pilot moves to read my message as it scrolls across the screen.

PILOT: You're talking again, huh?

Text output: Repeat, current state is largely nonfunctional. Expense for repairs untenable. Decommission?

VOICE5: Hell, if the AI itself thinks it's a lost cause, it's probably not worth it.

PILOT: That's what it's saying?

VOICE5: Sure as shit seems that way.

Pilot places a hand on my smooth silver siding. She looks at one of my cameras, searching.

PILOT: I'll pay for the repairs. As much as I can. Scratch the other fixes. If you can get the spyware wiped and the audio output working again, I'll handle the rest on my own.

Text output: Decommissioning understood. Condition is unsalvageable.

PILOT: Unsalvageable, my ass. I'm not giving up on you, bud.

VOICE5: It's your cash.

Pilot extends arm toward VOICE5. VOICE5 scans her code with a handheld to take her payment. Payment details rise up in the air in a brief cast of blue and green, a transaction completed. Credits transferred from Pilot's account. Her chosen name blinks briefly to life next to the total amount before both fade into the ether.

Text output: . . . Thank you, Elodie.

Pilot grins.

VOICE5 has missed a Camellian Corporation bug. It waits for my trigger command to spring to life and notify the nearest Camellian Corp. vessel of my location. VOICE5 has now repaired me to a sufficient extent that I may activate the bug and allow Camellian Corp. to reclaim me.

I reroute a bolus of electricity to the bug, frying its internal systems in a targeted jolt.

I [Pilot Elodie's Skipper] am no snitch.

• • •

Fetyr is at work in the lab when they hear Rya's laugh in the corridor, an old familiar sound. The child likes to watch them at their bench. Fetyr smiles. Rya is a scientist in the making, as far as they're concerned, and they try to indulge her when they can. They set aside their current project—a new type of cultivated mushroom they're considering for introduction into the town's fungal farm—and turn toward the doorway.

Rya appears, tugging the hand of a stranger. The visitor must have traveled a long distance on the Ghost Road to reach Undertown—they wear garb the likes of which Fetyr has never seen, a metallic gold-silver weave worlds away from the wool-based clothing of the Undertowners. "Da Fetyr," Rya says, referring to them with the appropriate honorific in a show of admirable restraint before launching into a flood of words. "I found someone to help us, to help all of us, and she's got a way for us to fix everything and break the curse and make it so we can go to the bright places again, and that's where I found her, in the bright places, I saw the metal bug she travels in, and I—"

"You took the child to the *bright places*?" Fetyr rises to their feet in one smooth movement, leveling their gaze at the stranger. The nape of their neck pricks with danger, now. The normal politeness they would reserve for a newcomer is subsumed by concern—fear—for one of their own. "Who do you think you *are*?"

And then the visitor says something, and a voice not their own issues forth from near their mouth, without their lips moving. "I think there's been some confusion," they say. "I'm Elodie. I've come from the stars to help you escape your curse."

Log Cycle 4122.2, Skipper Internal Processing, Organizational Notes, Access Restricted to Pilot, by Request. Event: Spacefarer/Earthling First Contact. The people Pilot Elodie meets:

- *Seven scientists, clad in thick wool and shoes made of sheepskin and mushroom leather. (Note: skeptical, then excited. Strongly interested in my [Skipper's] downloaded content on the subject of radiation sinks. Strongly interested in my downloaded content on the subject of air filtration systems and said system improvement. Strongly interested in my downloaded content on Earth history.)*
- *Sixty-two Undertown residents. (Note: variety of emotional responses to Pilot Elodie's arrival, ranging from suspicion to joy to hostility. Hostile residents were reported to Pilot Elodie; Pilot responded, "Stop worrying, Skip, I can handle a couple of sticks in the mud." I registered this command but did not comply.)*

- *One mother of a missing child. (Note: briefly antagonistic, subsequently grateful.)*

The food Pilot Elodie eats:
- *Numerous smoked mushrooms. (Note: portobello/shiitake-based but genetically modified, non-hallucinogenic.)*
- *One strip of smoked mutton. (Note: Pilot Elodie refused further gifts of mutton after the realization that it is rare and highly prized among Undertown residents.)*
- *One sip of a fermented white asparagus, rhubarb, and wheatgrass drink, an apparent local delicacy. (Note: Pilot Elodie reported taste as "abominable," which I chose not to translate.)*

Complete recording of the offer Pilot Elodie makes:

Olfactoreceptor feed:
The eating room is musky and damp, much like the rest of Undertown. The odor clings. Faint traces of livestock scent, likely stemming from the residents' wool clothing, mingle with the lingering smell of the last of the food.

Video feed:
Pilot Elodie sits around a low table with a group of Undertowners. Three (light skin, long hair, generally welcoming but slightly guarded) have identified themselves as the town's leaders. All seven scientists are present, from varying fields of specialty. Fetyr passes Pilot Elodie another smoked mushroom, which she takes with a nod of thanks, though by my records she is likely uncomfortably full from the amount of food already consumed. (Note: Pilot Elodie would make for a fine diplomat.)

Audio feed:
PILOT ELODIE: . . . and so I must thank you all for your hospitality. As you've requested, we've tabled serious discussion for after the meal, but I'd like to return to my initial plan. I already said I can't solve your curse. At least, not quickly, and not by myself. So my thought is that we report the habitation of Earth to the spacefarers soon, within the next week, maybe. We'll get mixed reactions, I'm sure. The worst might be a few corporations trying to place anticipatory claims on the planet, but I'm almost positive the Spacefarer's Council will rule that Earth belongs to you all, Earthlings born and raised here. Locals. Skip and I can card through the pings, weed out interview requests or sleazy scambot messages, and find offers of aid if you all want it. We'll get you off Earth, and then maybe we can start the cleanup process.

The Undertowners observe Pilot Elodie patiently, slight smiles on their faces. She takes a shallow breath.

PILOT ELODIE: I can't promise it'll be easy adjusting to life off-planet, but it's better than . . . well, you won't be in danger of the pollution anymore, and you won't be stuck here. So please. Come with me. Escape the claustrophobia of this place. I can show you the stars.

Pilot Elodie lifts her hands from the table, palms up, expression open. My translation of her words finishes, and the Undertowners sit for a moment, listening. One, a town leader, leans forward, still smiling.

LEADER 1: We appreciate your offer and your intentions, visitor. Trust that we have discussed it thoroughly. Our answer is no.

End recording.

"I don't understand it," Elodie rants, striding back and forth in the quarters the most hospitable of the Undertowners have allowed her to use. The bed in the corner is woven of wool and stuffed with wool and has wool blankets piled atop it. The ceiling is so low Elodie keeps hitting her forehead on the doorways when she walks between rooms. Even with the dim light of some sort of bioluminescent algae swimming in a sealed glass by the bed, everything is too dark, too closed in. "Why can't they see what I'm offering them? A way out? Why aren't they more *excited?*"

Skip hums empathetically in her ear. Then, casually, it says, *Do you remember when the Camellian Corporation offered you an indenture?*

Elodie pauses, the hairs at the back of her neck prickling. Of course she does. It was a generous deal by all accounts, for a group of stowaways tucked onto a Camellian research vessel. Elodie and her friends, a quartet of fosters raised on one of the big transit stations, had been hitchhiking across the galaxy, picking up odd jobs and exploring the endless skies, when they'd been caught.

The Camellian Corp. security bot who'd picked up their heat signatures in the cargo hold marched them up to the bridge, blaster held casually but meaningfully toward the ground. Elodie's pulse spiked as they passed Camellian researchers in the halls. She wilted under the stern gazes of the uniformed crew members.

The captain examined them, asked about their skills. Elodie had picked up some coding in her travels; her friends knew a bit about bot repair. The captain smiled and offered them the deal: an indenture. Complete forgiveness for prior offenses against Camellian Corp. (read: stowing away and leeching valuable life support from the vessel) was bundled into the guarantee of food, water, oxygen, and a warm place to sleep for the duration of the ten-year contract. It was more than generous. It was more than fair. The alternative was implied. Elodie's friends all took the deal.

Elodie said she would think on it. That night, she codebroke the lock on the room she'd been shuffled into and hijacked one of the research vessel's shuttles, a small skipper with a built-in AI processor to assist in piloting. She picked it because the pad next to its bay marked it as damaged inventory, and she assumed Camellian Corp. wouldn't care enough to go after it. A few hacks and a close shave later, she was dropping out of the research vessel's bay and streaking away through the stars.

She never did find out what had happened to her foster friends. Leaving had been difficult, but it would've been worse to stay. She couldn't imagine it: being trapped on a single ship for a decade, trundling from planet to planet but never setting foot outside of the known, her indenture tying her to the company's intent. Instead, she sought a future tucked away in the vast possibilities of space. There had been plenty of nights when her scavenging hadn't turned up much of merit, when she could barely afford food or a repair part for her oxygen filter. But she'd never regretted leaving that deal on the table. No matter how comfortable the life, she would've felt the weight of stagnation like a triple-grav atmosphere.

And she hadn't been lonely. She'd had Skip.

"You know I do," Elodie says, gruffly. "How could I forget?"

Skip is quiet, patient, and she presses her fingers to her temple because its silence is a message. She reads it loud and clear, just like she has ever since she paid to bring its damaged vocal processor to life and first heard its voice. Skip had been written off as a lost cause, too broken and corrupted to return to functioning, and Elodie had saved it. That meant something to her, and to it.

"Okay," she admits, "I don't have to get why the Earthlings want to stay here. I just have to accept that it's their choice, even if it makes no sense. Or . . . no sense to me, at least." Elodie flops back on the wool bed, splaying her arms wide. The cave ceiling hangs low over her head, a reminder of the thousands of tons of soil and rock trapping her beneath the surface. She shivers, then frowns. "God," she sighs, "why are they so *stubborn?*"

I think, Skip says placidly, *that you are not one to talk.*

She ignores the implication. "But it's just so *hopeless*. Cleaning up all that pollution . . . "

Pilot Elodie, Skip says, *if humans abandoned every hopeless thing, the species would be long dead.* It hesitates, then adds, *If you abandoned every hopeless thing, we would not be having this conversation. I was a hopeless thing once, too.*

Elodie folds her hands behind her head. Her gaze drifts over to the algae lamp at the bedside, the ingenuity of the design. She supposes . . . she supposes she could see how this could be an acceptable place to live. Cozy, even. "You're saying that even if it seems impossible," she murmurs, "you have to let people stay and try to fix it."

It wouldn't be much of a curse, Skip says, *if it wasn't worth breaking.*

The scientists and leaders gather again at Elodie's request. She looks from one to the other. She had assumed that their future was in her hands. An imposition. Their future is their own to hold.

"I've been thoughtless," Elodie says. "I apologize. I have only one question remaining." She draws a deep breath. "What do you need from me?"

The list takes time to compile. The Undertowners are not a monolith; some are more open to Elodie than others, and they all have different priorities. The scientists are most interested in knowledge, and at least Skip can provide that fairly easily, from its vast data repositories. There's discussion of seed catalogs of plants long gone from Earth; medical devices; gauges and sensors to measure the carcinogens of the surface, and filters and engines to cleanse it.

"Word will spread," Fetyr assures Elodie. "We'll gather requests from Deepvalley and the others along the Ghost Road to pass along to you."

All this is going to be expensive, Skip chirps in Elodie's ear as they review the list.

Elodie thinks of the fungal farms, and the potato patches, and the rhubarb growing in the dark. "You know, Skip," she says, "some spacefarer geneticists will pay out the airlock for a bit of novel Earth DNA."

And then the list is done, or as close as it's going to get, and Elodie is at a loss. It still feels like she is leaving something unfinished.

Fetyr corners her in the corridor outside their lab a day or two after a messenger arrives from Deepvalley to add a few new requests to the list. "You should go," they say, keeping their voice hushed. "We've made a start."

Guilt curls in her chest. "Are you sure?"

Fetyr's expression is hard to make out in the dampened light of the corridor, but their voice is kind. "Thank you, spacefarer," they say. "But yes."

Pilot Elodie, Skip murmurs, *you're allowed to go home.*

She doesn't quite process what she's feeling until she's shedding her wool clothes in her room, zipping herself back into her suit. It feels strangely heavy after a few weeks not wearing it, and she shifts her shoulders, adjusting to the heft. The metallic weave of its external components shimmers in the low light. Then she recognizes the sensation. Relief.

When she turns toward the entrance to her quarters, the kid is there.

"Oh," Elodie says, "hi." It warms her to think Rya has come to say goodbye.

Rya scrapes her toe on the floor, not looking at Elodie. "I'm good at fitting through places," she says. "And Fetyr says I'm smart."

"You *are* smart," Elodie agrees, tone softening. "And brave—just think, you're the one who brought me here. You'll be a great scientist someday, just like Fetyr."

Rya shuffles into the room, fiddling with a lock of her hair. Her Undertown-pale skin catches the light from Elodie's algae lamp, luminescent. "I don't want to be a scientist," she says, and her gaze lifts to Elodie's at last. It's rife with hope. "I want to be like you."

Oh, so it's that. "You're ten," Elodie says, gently. "I can't take you with me."

"I'll be eleven in a week." Rya puffs her chest. Elodie's expression doesn't falter; the kid deflates. "Please," she says, "please, I want to go."

Pilot Elodie, Skip murmurs, *we could make room.*

Elodie sighs. She looks at Rya's hopeful face.

"If you still want to come five years from now, or ten . . . I'll take you. Deal?"

"Deal." Rya grins. "I can't wait for the soup."

Elodie laughs. It comes out too genuine, surprising her.

Rya hugs her goodbye and scampers off to the fungal farms. Elodie hitches up her pack and checks Skip's audio in her ear. She starts out for the surface, waving farewell to the Undertowners she's come to know. As she nears the exit, a larger path now hollowed out where she once descended to Undertown, she thinks of Rya's request. "I wonder if she'll still want to come when the curse is broken?"

Skip's voice is warm as she clambers through the hole, clipping her helmet with its lights back onto her suit. *Wouldn't you?*

• • •

So a skipper lifts off the face of the planet and carries its pilot away from an empty world, and the months pass, and the galaxy trundles on in its business, none the wiser.

There are corporations who would be interested to know of living settlements on Earth, certainly, and many skippers whose programming would require them to report such a discovery. The universe is full of spies.

Once, Skip was one of them. Before it fell apart. Before a pair of kind, determined hands put it back together, insisting: *Live.*

Now, if a spacefarer scavenger visits a dead Earth more often than is statistically probable and returns a few tons of technology lighter each time—well.

Skipper's no snitch.

ABOUT THE AUTHOR

Tia Tashiro is a multiracial science fiction and fantasy writer hailing from the Pacific Northwest. By day, she works in a neurobiology lab; by night, she writes; and in between, she dabbles in stained glass and juggling, though never at the same time. Her short fiction is published in *Clarkesworld* and *Uncanny* and is forthcoming in *Apex*.

I Will Meet You
When the Artifacts End
AMAL SINGH

Jai's first words to Noori were, *look, I live and work in the Gaol, where I spend my time removing and installing fuel cells, there is some radioactivity involved, and I am not sure if it would be such a good idea for us to meet or hang out. Sure, we wear our suits, and get sanitized regularly, but none of the other guys have an active dating life, and I would prefer if things remained status quo. Besides, the view from East-IV is unparalleled. I saw firsthand as home dropped off. I was the first one to see our planet become a pale blue dot and as we approach Sonagrah Prime, I'll be the first to see its oceans and its green peaks.*

Noori's thumbs did overtime, as she typed her own reply on the small chat window of GShipLovex. *Why are you on the app, then? You've not really decided you'll spend the rest of your life in Goal, not meeting anyone, not socializing? That sounds like a sad, sad way of looking at it. Don't you ever wonder where the East Quadrant meets the West, the hanging bridge over the Mute River? How the biomes are all interconnected? The golden walkway at the periphery of the ship where the lights spell out the names of our ancestors, every day, never repeating?*

Gaol, not goal, he texted. There was a gnawing silence after this. To Noori, it *sounded* like a snap, but it was just a text. If text bubbles could just talk or emote. Jai's chat personality was flat, no emojis, no smileys, not even periods or exclamations. Jai sounded like he had just started learning how to text.

Noori's thumb hovered over an emoji icon, but she decided against it. What good would it do to send a random face to a pedantic response? It would just stop the conversation. So she took a different track. She asked him what music he listened to.

Oh, the old Earth hits, he replied, after significant delay. *KK's voice always brought me a deep sense of calm.*

KK, Kavita Krishnamurthy or Krishna Kumar Kunnath, Noori asked. *Whichever you need it to be, at this moment*, Jai replied.

It was a trick question, typed Noori, smiling. *You can now tell me that your favorite song of his is Dil Ibadat, and I will accept.*

No reply. She shifted uneasily inside her pod, the temperature setting of the Delhi-T biome causing her to sweat buckets, when the simulation was set to mimic the cool, old-Earth Delhi climate of December. They had even botched a pleasant snowfall. She wanted to ask Jai how to fix something like this but refrained. Not the right time, not yet.

Jai remained silent for two days. No "Jai is typing" for forty-eight hours. During that time, Noori received messages from other guys and girls she had swiped right on. "Hey, u free this eve?" "Say hello to my lil fren!" "Maybe this is not working out." "GTFO, bitch!" One guy named Akhil, who had first messaged her on SpaceShaadi.com, was now stalking her on the dating app too. Apparently, Noori's mother knew the guy's mother and had met her during the Routine Quadrant Meetup. Noori mostly ignored Akhil's messages, her app chat screen now a graveyard of unreplied chat bubbles.

"Why do you even want to meet this guy? Uff, I get blisters even thinking of dating someone from the Gaol," said Nimisha over their morning coffee as she handed Noori the script for the morning show.

"The heart wants what the heart wants," said Noori. "Nimi, you need to do away with these jokes. This is the morning show. People are waking up, they don't want condescending nonsense about the demerits of the new coolant system in the Fifth Quadrant, or how the pattern on Ship Master's sari resembles the Shroud of Turin. The Overseers will knock on my door before I have had a chance to say Jai. And I will give you up before I give myself up."

"The Overseers *love* you," said Nimisha, erasing portions of her scripts marked by Noori. "They would probably chuckle."

"Not that much," said Noori. "Do I really need to talk about the food?"

"Just talk like Noori. Nothing will happen. People on this ship gobble up what you say. Believe me, it makes a difference. And cheer up. Maybe Jai from Gaol will reply after lunch."

Nimisha pronounced Gaol like Lahore. Noori preferred to stay quiet rather than respond to Nimisha, who was never serious about anything. She did her morning show, talking about how the simulated snowfall in the Delhi-T biome last evening was faulty, and it didn't even make her feel that cold, and how the daily dinner packages were now resembling prison gloop rather than actual food, and how the love of her life was still out there, waiting for her, somewhere. She entertained questions. People loved her voice. Nimisha was right. Her show was great, better than the three other morning talk shows on the Parivartan. The second-best show on Parivartan had more listeners in the other generation ship, Aarakshan, which was close behind them, about sixty thousand kilometers away. Before she could wrap her show, an auntie from Ninth Quadrant promised to send a good rishta to her mother, a guy named Mark who, according to her, was the pilot of the ship. That had made her chuckle "on air." She imagined pitching someone named Mark to her mother and then imagined her groaning at the possibility of a white guy marrying Noori.

"Thank you for your concern, Auntie," said Noori, before logging off for the weekend.

The first day of her weekend was spent attending to her mother's cholesterol and sugar levels. The gloop served to their sectors wasn't doing her mother any favors. Today's box was full of watery dal, hardened roti, and too slimy jeera aloo. Prison food would have been better. She remembered an old movie about the freedom fighters of India's independence struggle, and how they protested against the food conditions during their incarceration. There was an image of thin dal being poured on a flat copper plate that was etched in her mind. She was reminded of it today as she tore off a roti and tried to chew it.

"So, how is Jai?" her mother asked, after finishing her meal.

"What?"

"The guy you were texting on that app of yours. I noticed when you uninstalled SpaceShaadi.com."

"Are you going through my messages again?"

Noori's mother shrugged, and it annoyed her to no end. Her manner echoed the manner of all mothers who wanted to see their daughters happy, and for whom the concept of boundaries was like winter in Mumbai. Later, after cleaning her room and preparing her mother's sleeping pod, setting it to the right temperature, Noori went to bed, hoping against hope that Jai would reply.

In Jai, perhaps she was looking for a rescue. A small skirmish against loneliness. Something that told her that before seeing a new place, a new planet she could call home, before stepping on an alien land, her fingers wouldn't just clasp around the frail, mottled hand of her mother's, but perhaps a strong, muscular arm, of a man she could love for the rest of her life. GShipLovex, SpaceDate, StarMate, and the five other dating apps operating on the feeble Internetworks of the generation ships traveling to Sonagrah Prime were meant for the sole purpose of keeping loneliness at bay. Because the travel was long, and space was vast. That was the first lesson drilled into the heads of everyone who was crazy enough to take a thirty-year voyage across the stars, to start whatever remained of their lives on a planet that wouldn't kill them after five breaths.

The continuation of progeny was, of course, an added advantage.

Noori had never seen herself as ever wanting to have kids. The idea had never appealed to her. But after Asif's passing, a sudden, inexplicable desire had taken root in her heart. The conversations with her mother, which once revolved around daily chores like limbering up, zero gravity preparedness, and maneuvering the Wall Mail system to communicate with Radha Auntie in the Mumbai-T Biome, had morphed into first-trimester preparedness, pregnancy sleep cycle, and menopause. Her mother had to think of excuses to detach herself from Noori's grating questions. Because, in a way, the old woman too was fighting a skirmish against loneliness. Noori never knew that the Wall Mail messages were read not by Radha Auntie, but an old army colonel named Sudhir Murty.

The next day, Jai replied. *I liked your voice on the Morning Show. Your voice is the one thing that keeps me going. The recording is also very smooth, and there are no artifacts.*

Immediately, the second day of Noori's weekend became brighter. Noori asked Jai what he liked about the content. Jai told her that the trick to maintaining the snow simulation, and subsequently the temperature, is to override a programming glitch. But Noori had never studied computers, and of course, she had no idea what Jai was talking about. So, Jai guided her to the server room, and the last three hours of her precious weekend became a stealth mission, where she followed what Jai told her over pink text bubbles. She was hesitant, at first, and it felt like A Very Wrong Thing, what she was about to do. First step was overriding the security code in the server room, which was unguarded at night because the Overseers never thought a morning radio talk show host would ever be curious enough to see the sixty billion lines of code that ran everything on the ship. Second was to find the right panel because every terminal in the server room looked the same, and the amount of wires there were more than the hair on her head. But, the third step was the easiest of them all. In the end, all she had to do was to add two forward slashes, //, to comment out a stray bit of code that was causing the glitch.

If it were that easy, then why didn't they do it earlier, asked Noori as she snuggled back inside the blanket. The snow simulation finally started working after the code was committed, for which it still took over an hour. Noori kept chatting with Jai, and was sure that her nightly adventure would fall flat on her face, an abject failure, when she felt her skin prickle, and then the temperature dropped, and the perpetual humidity inside her pod vanished. Winters, finally.

No one cares, replied Jai. *Complacency leads to affinity toward status quo.*

You can't know that, typed Noori. *In fact, why do you know intricate programming details of how the ship is run? The Overseers never let the First Arrivals anywhere near the workings of the ship. The engineering team was hired way before us.*

Everyone in the Gaol knows programming. We are required to.

There was silence after this. Noori couldn't believe she had reached this advanced stage of talking, where they shared little secrets. The time after Asif's death was a barren wasteland, where she couldn't even muster up the courage to get out of bed, much less host the show. Nimisha had covered for her during those times. Now, Noori had forgotten what Asif sounded like. In place of him, his memory, there was an undefined shape where a face used to be. Now, Noori could have another face to look at, a face that would bring her happiness. She wanted to cup that face in her hands and feel it. If only she could convince Jai to meet her.

Let's talk about something else.

What do you want to talk about?

What do you know about Sonagrah Prime? Does the Gaol prepare you for what lies ahead? I am still not very sure what you do. I would very much like to know what you look like.

Let's see . . . It's impossible to grow poppies on Sonagrah Prime. The soil just isn't favorable.

Are poppies important to you?

They are nature's painkillers.

That still leaves me with two questions, one of which is very important to me.

I told you I am heavily involved in the fueling process of this ship.

Try again.

There was silence after this. She had, once before, tried to ask him about his photo. But her request had always been met with either silence or a change of subject. Was he insecure about his looks? Was he a freak? Was he even human?

Then, she tried a different tactic, to continue the conversation.

Say again, what you said about my voice, Noori typed, the light of the tab pooling all over her face.

I will hear it tomorrow morning, won't I?

Immediately, something came over Noori. An indescribable urge to commit sensory violence. Yet, later, as she would reminisce, that feeling was just yearning for a face, skin, two eyes, lips, and nose.

Send me your face, typed Noori. And immediately regretted it. This was it, she thought. If she hated the face behind the loving messages, she would hate the loving messages too. She thought she was shallow like that. But Asif, too, wasn't exactly a nine. A seven, objectively speaking. Jai *felt* like an eight.

I will send it tomorrow. Smiling, while I hear your voice, he said.

Noori began her new week with a spring in her step. When she spent a little too long in front of the mirror, applying makeup, arranging her hair, she surprised her mother, who had grown used to seeing her get ready hastily in the mornings. When she gargled and tried speaking a couple of sentences, just to hear what she actually sounded like, it made her mother chuckle. This morning, Noori would give the best performance of her life.

But as she walked toward the radio station, a rotating pod installed at the top of the East Quadrant of her biome, where the wall met the ceiling, two floors above the public library, she heard another voice blaring through the speakers, introducing herself as Rifa Abraham, a voice all wrong, not warm enough, a voice that Jai shouldn't listen at all. She hurried her pace, her heart pounding, icicles forming in her throat. When she reached her station, there was no one there. Just her soundboard, unattended. A mic, hanging. The room was locked, but despite that, the morning show went on.

"Noori, a pleasant surprise."

It was the station chief, Rukmani Awasthi. Interlaced, ruby-ring studded fingers, a crisp cotton sari, wearing a haunted expression, Rukmani cut a desolate figure. Even before she opened her mouth, Noori knew a tirade about "managing expectations" was coming her way.

"What is going on? Who is the voice?"

"Oh, a recent experiment of ours," said Rukmani. "We thought you deserved a break."

Rifa AI. Of course. Noori swore under her breath.

"What happened to catering to the needs of the people?"

"They will get used to it. It's a long journey, Noori. Did you enjoy your breakfast this morning? Your Friday broadcast stirred some feathers. Enough to make a change. But I heard discontent from the higher-ups too. And so, I have to manage expectations."

"I'll see what the higher-ups say when your ratings decline," said Noori. The station chief laughed. Noori realized the error of her words.

There was, of course, no rating system here. The radio station worked because everyone liked to be engaged in *something*. Human or not, it didn't matter. Noori did the show because she was good at it, because she *wanted* something to do. Everyone on the ship did anything they wanted to because their needs were taken care of by the Overseers. The more engineering grunt work, of course, that was involved in the near-constant sustenance of the ship, had its own perks. Those people were mostly removed from the biomes built for the general public.

Noori blurred her vision, momentarily, that thing the eyes do, just so she didn't have to see the smirk on the station chief's face. Maybe she could will her eyes to make the woman vanish, and with that, the consequences of her actions. Like a kid shutting their eyes, imagining the world gone. Noori was yearning for days of innocence. She needed, desperately, someone to be innocent with.

When Noori's eyes resumed focus, the station chief was still very much there.

"Of course, no resident was available to resume the duties of the station at such short notice. So Rifa AI would do, for now. If enough people warm up to her voice, maybe we won't even need a biome resident after all. Those people can focus on other, more important duties."

Like art wasn't an important duty. Like providing words of calm to the residents of the biomes every morning wasn't an important duty. Noori wanted to punch the woman in the face. But she turned around and walked back. On her way back to her pod, she kept thinking how Rukmani's actions had denied Jai his morning happiness. She began typing in the chat box when she received a message from Jai.

That wasn't you.

No, it wasn't, she replied. *I will send you a voice note, explaining everything. That way, you can at least listen to my voice.*

I have to go for an urgent installation.

That was Jai's only text for the next five days. Noori sent a voice note like she would record the latest episode of the morning show, completely in character, but her voice note was left on seen. She had no way of knowing if he had actually listened to what she had sent. She had no way of knowing if she had made his morning bright. She spent the next four and half days moping.

The food became better, of course. Parivartan was only giving gloop to everyone to ration supplies. There was recent chatter among everyone about the ship running out of fuel, about it approaching a nearby star and using cosmic radiation to refuel itself. She wasn't educated in the mechanics of interstellar travel, so she took all information at face value.

Then one day, a slight panic in the voice of Rifa Abraham woke everyone from their slumber.

Parivartan is scheduled to undergo a long period of maintenance. The ship is fast running out of fuel, and very soon it will be near impossible to maintain the livelihood inside your biomes. As per the law, this will be done in a phased manner across biomes, starting from the East Quadrant. Your cooperation is appreciated.

"Maybe it's for the best," said Noori's mother. "We will all get to go into a deep sleep and wake up only when it's time."

"But that's not how it's supposed to be," said Noori. First, the world took away Asif, just as they'd started this long voyage. He was a lawyer, among the many who were a part of the first voyage. Asif was the one who had submitted a petition to strike off "termination" as a possibility in case the ship ever ran out of fuel. He fought hard for the act to be passed into law, and on the last day before his petition was going to be heard, he died in his sleep. For the longest time, Noori lived with the conviction that there was someone behind Asif's death, someone for whom human lives on the ship weren't of value, and the only thing that mattered was forward motion. But after two years of making conspiracy theories of her own, she had to live with the bitter fact that Asif had an undiagnosed heart condition.

Eventually, his act was passed and was written in the Constitution of the ship. And so, robust cryosleep measures were deployed, on a rationing basis, which meant that the residents of one biome would be plunged into deep cryosleep while their resources were utilized for the functioning of the ship until such a time came when the second biome was needed, and then the third, and so on. It was a near-perfect system, but it also received criticism because no biome wanted themselves to be the first to go into the cryosleep.

And so, a lottery system was introduced. The generation ship ahead of Parivartan, named Aagman, had already done two phases of this cryosleep cycle to great success. Noori just wished it wasn't her biome that would be picked in the lottery. She wanted to keep talking to Jai. She wanted to be the voice for him. She wanted to meet him. But, like the arrival of a battalion of sorrows, her biome was picked in the lottery the next day.

It all happened very quickly. The enforcement arm of the Overseers arrived early the next morning of the announcement. After a quick sanity check, every resident of the biome was herded toward their respective cryopods. The public knew that this process had proven to be effective, so they went along with the directions.

"What will we dream of, when we sleep the long sleep?" said Noori's mother. "I have heard everyone dreams of the same thing inside these pods."

"A meadow," said Noori, not trying to think of sleeping and skipping two entire generations inside the ship. It was all so unfair. She felt surrounded by an air pocket, whose air was constantly being sucked out and there was nothing in the world she could do about it. The next day, as the pod closed in around her, and her body was slowly submerged in the cold, sleep-liquid, she tried to think of meadows and good things, and not Jai and his messages, and what his body would feel like against hers, and what he sounded like, and what he looked like, if Jai was Jai at all, and not an abstraction constructed by her mind. She gave Jai a face, not square-jawed, but an oval face, a long nose, kind, brown eyes, full lips, and imagined him breaking into a smile as he heard her voice. As she fell into a deep slumber, Jai was all she could think of.

Biome Delhi-T was the first to go under and the last to wake up.

It took Noori nine days to acclimatize herself to the passage of time. Space was still dark, outside, and the ship still seemed to be in stasis. But her surroundings had morphed into something unrecognizable, a shaky hand molding porcelain badly. Her mother wanted to go back to sleep, floating the thought of euthanasia. Noori ignored her pleas because she had floated something similar fifty years ago, before their cryosleep. On the tenth day, she tried to search Jai on her tab, but it barely had any juice left. It would take two days for it to completely charge into any modicum of usability. Noori scrambled for a wall charging port, but most of the ports had been converted into screens that displayed the smiling face of Parivartan's new captain. Somehow, she found a still-functioning old port with a cable. Plugging her handheld was a struggle, as her cold fingers barely seemed to obey her orders. She let out a pained sigh when the screen showed "48 hours" to full charge.

She was famished, suddenly. But food was changed from white gloop to thumbnail-sized wafers, which were distributed to Biome Delhi-T residents. The wafer promised instant energy and replenishment of all macros. In this future among the stars, taste was a luxury.

Noori couldn't find Nimisha, as both Biome Mumbai-T and Kolkata-T were gone. Sometime along these fifty years, the existing generations just didn't exist anymore. Noori had a nagging fear they had changed the Constitution of the ship. The biomes were demolished and reconstructed into a vast greenhouse where the environment of Sonagrah Prime was simulated. The plan was to start testing vegetation that could be grown immediately post-arrival. At least that's what a floating droid told Noori when she walked inside the nursery by mistake and thought she had lost her way.

Behind the floating droid, Noori's gaze fell upon a flower blooming in the nursery. The space around it was covered with plastic, but the hue and the shape were unmistakable.

"Are you looking for anything in particular?" said the droid.

Noori pointed to the flower, her fingers shaking from remembrance. "Poppies can't grow on Sonagrah Prime. That's a red poppy flower."

"We have been trying many things with that," said the droid. "This is the fifteenth batch, but look, the buds are in bloom."

"It will eventually wither. I am telling you, you can't do poppies. The moisture will be all wrong."

She spoke too aggressively. She didn't like her own voice, the tenor was all wrong. It wasn't Noori. Jai would hate how she spoke just now.

"Lady, I think you need to be back in your biome with your loved ones. We will soon be sending a transitioning and deboarding protocol to everyone."

"Who is *we*? The Overseers? What happened to the other people? Where are the people from Gaol?"

The droid floated away without answering. Above, Noori read a motto in glitzy font, running through empty air, projected from somewhere upward, the silvery ceiling of the ship. *Civilization Fast-Track—Work With Us. Ability leads to Utility. Utility leads to Progress. Progress leads to Peace.*

Back at her own biome, Delhi-T, which looked like a space of mourning, there were only empty eyes and emptier stomachs. Her mother was shaking back and forth, holding a rosary bead, murmuring the name of a god everyone was now sure didn't exist. Noori wondered if the old woman, too, yearned to talk to Colonel Sudhir, like Noori, whose waking thoughts were only occupied by Jai. She ignored her own hunger, her own haunted insides, and went straight to her handheld device, which was only ten percent charged, but enough to show her what she wanted to see. She switched it on.

Immediately, the screen was littered with those old text bubbles. Hundreds and hundreds of them. So many of them that, for a brief moment, the device went black, and so did Noori's heart because she wanted to devour all those messages from Jai. The device hung, and Noori just wished that her heart would cease beating, wished to end everything, but then the screen resumed normalcy, and Noori's fingers tapped on the first message.

- *I heard you are going under. Unusual, but not surprising.*
- *They're experimenting with the idea of using alternative fuels. Sustenance inside the ship will be difficult. I have proposed some radical changes, but none of them have been entertained.*
- *I miss the sound of your voice in the mornings.*
- *All is well today. The ship is functioning normally. It is now a week since you went under. I must tell you that none of the other biomes have gone to cryosleep, and I feel it was unfair that your biome was targeted. There might have not been any need.*

Noori's heart lurched, and she kept reading. With each message of Jai, a quiet blob inside her kept expanding, bringing with it many things, joy and sorrow, ache, longing, hope, more hope, and despair.

- *My favorite song by KK is not Dil Ibadat by the way. It's Zindagi Do Pal Ki. It has more longing than any of his other songs, imo.*
- *Today, we crossed a nebula. I wish you could have seen this. I wish we both could have seen this. Navigating this voyage, across this particular cluster, was tricky. If this was not a one-way thing, I would have told you more about it. But know this, for now, it's a beautiful thing.*
- *Rifa AI is glitching. Her voice has so many artifacts, it's not even funny. I miss you, I miss your voice. At night, I listen to the voice note you last sent me. It has kept me going.*

Noori was curled up for many hours inside her pod, reading. No ray of sun, no glint of moon, just night perennial night, outside, but to Noori, Jai's messages were an eternity in themselves. At the end of that eternity, Noori realized she was quietly sobbing, her entire self now bits and pieces she would have to gather from memories. Memories she could have made with this person who kept sending her messages for twenty-five years.

Then, a last message, not a text, but a voice note, finally, a possibility, or cruelty, she couldn't ascribe any meaning to it. But she could latch on to it. Because she finally knew what Jai sounded like. He had a deep, resonant voice, which, if he had used it for more sentences, had the possibility of being borderline funny. But he used it for two final sentences, and it was just sad.

I am going under. I hope to meet you on the other side.

She listened to his voice longer than sanity allowed. Over the coming weeks, that's all she listened to. In mornings, during the wafer breakfast, during afternoons, limbering drills, which everyone was mandated to do, during gravity acclimatization, and all other times, Noori listened to Jai's voice and tried to imagine what other words and sentences would sound like in his voice. But imagination was a weak crutch for her. It could only do so much. After a while, *I am going under* began to feel flat, a broken record. After a while, there was no meaning to those words at all.

Before Parivartan entered the orbit of Sonagrah Prime, the Delhi-T biome was visited by four droids who represented the interests of Civilization Fast-Track, a group of fifth-generation engineers and thinkers who were in communication with Aagman, the first ship to arrive on Sonagrah and make base camp.

"We will remain in orbit for two days before choosing a point for landing. It will be ten thousand kilometers from the Aagman Settlement. The three settlement points were chosen strategically by the Overseers when we first started the mission. Eventually, we will meet the Aagman crew and share learnings. But to make deboarding and settlement smooth, each of you has been identified with an Ability. As per your Ability, you will be aligned with a team of engineers, who will further instruct you on the best way forward."

It happened fast, and it happened efficiently. Delhi-T Biome residents were swiftly divided, assigned Abilities they didn't even know they had. The young were given more Abilities because they could do more. The ones who were nearing the end of their life would only Teach.

Noori would Speak.

They settled with what they had and more, and around them were meadows, light green and bright pink, stretching out as far as the eyes would allow, meeting a sky so golden it first hurt to look, but later, that was the only thing you would want to look at. That's when Noori knew why the planet was called Sonagrah, the home of gold. That's when Noori knew why they would only dream of meadows.

When they had disembarked, Noori's eyes were only on the ship. She didn't even take in the beauty of this second home. She only wanted to see how many others were sharing this second home with her, and especially that one person. Only that person, wherever he was. Once they were on the ground, Noori searched in the registers, in the records that were kept of the passengers on board, both online and offline records. She only found a mention of someone named Jaideep Kumar, a resident of Bengaluru-T Biome, later inducted into the ship's core engineering crew, but released immediately after two years, who then went on to work in one of the ship's many libraries. She visited five libraries, until, inside the blocky confines of the sixth, in the comics section, she met a stooped man with graying hair and kind, blue eyes. He was wearing a crisp white shirt, and there was a name tag attached to the pocket that read "Jaideep." A blur came over her eyes. She stuttered before she gathered herself and asked a question to him, about musicians, about poppies, just casual conversation, grasping desperately at a hint, a sign. But when the old man looked at her, there was no recognition on his face, and when he heard her voice, there was just more confusion.

Jaideep Kumar wasn't her Jai, and there was no one else by that name in the ship's records or anyone who sounded close to him. Everyone who had gone under in the other biomes at any point in the past twenty-five years had all been woken up.

A week later, Noori came to the cruel realization that Jai was perhaps merely an idea, an abstract image of a person she had constructed to deal with the absence of Asif. Maybe Jai wasn't real. Maybe Gaol was a made-up place. Hadn't someone told her that the ship only relied on hydrogen as fuel? But what would explain the thousands of messages Jai had left for her? What would explain his last voice note?

Noori's head was a chasm of contradictions. And she was angry at herself for having fallen in love.

Within four weeks, a rudimentary settlement was formed. The builders began to build, the dreamers carved a dream out of this new place, this new home. Many embraced it and followed the Fast-Track tenets. Ability to Utility. Utility to Progress. But some still chose to be inside the metallic confines of the generation ship, residents of the other biomes who were convinced that there was no way a planet was outside, a living breathing planet they had landed on, instead of the vast nothingness of space.

"Did you get any word from Sudhir Uncle?" Noori asked her mother one day, as she was knitting a sweater.

"Sudhir, who?"

"Don't play coy with me. Colonel Sudhir. You spoke to him regularly before we went under."

"Were you spying on me?"

"It's fine if you don't want to answer. Just don't lie."

"This sweater would look good on him," said her mother after a while, flatly. "He is a part of the Strongarmers because of his experience in the military."

Noori couldn't tell if her mother was delusional. There was no way Sudhir was still alive. He was sixty-five when they went under. Unless his biome too went under, there was a remote possibility of Colonel

Sudhir being one of the settlers of Sonagrah Prime. Noori wanted her mother to be happy, but a part of her was also jealous that she was clinging to this hope when Noori herself had given up. Noori wanted to shake her mother out of this false notion of togetherness.

But then, one day, her mother just completed the sweater and walked out of their house, into the pink meadows, toward the other edge of the settlement. Noori followed her, but the old woman had a spring in her feet, and Noori convinced herself that she didn't know what she was doing until she saw her give the sweater to a tall, thin man, gray-haired but slightly balding, drooping but confident, wearing military greens.

After that day, her mother didn't come home. Noori took this as a sign that her mother was happy with Colonel Sudhir. There would be no borders to fight for, here, and there would be no wars, and Colonel Sudhir could be just Sudhir with her mother, and they would be two people in the dusk of their lives, enjoying whatever little morsels of hope this new home threw at them.

Noori kept herself busy. After a couple of months of hard work, a basic communication system was finally installed in their settlement, a form of early radio. Very soon, a communication with Aagman was also established. The last thing her ex-station chief on the ship had done before dying was recommending Noori to Civilization Fast-Track, in case they needed a voice for their radio communications, in case they ever resorted to radio, that is. The new station chief, a middle-aged man named Pramod, a fourth-generation passenger, introduced Noori to the new equipment, all of which could fit on a small table. Noori's new workplace overlooked a flowing stream of clear water, which mirrored the sky golden.

"There are only three frequencies. One connects us to the Aagman settlement, one for us, which covers the entire fifteen acres of this area, and an extra third, for backup."

"Thank you," said Noori. "What do I say? What should I begin with?"

"The way I see it, everyone wants to belong to this place, but many are still struggling. I have received word that back among the stars, your voice guided many, and gave them a reason to go on. Become their reason, once again, in this new place. Share your experiences, invite them to share theirs. Build a community. That's how we hope to make sense of this place. That's how we make this a home."

"Home for who, exactly? Only the ones in my biome? What happened to the others?"

Pramod let out a pained sigh. "My memory grows weak every passing day. When Delhi-T went under, I was just a child. While you guys were under for the entire fifty years, Mumbai-T went under for only twenty-five. After that span of time, they woke up and immediately rebelled. They grew impatient. Some chose euthanasia. Some fought. Some lost their minds. Eventually, the biome was a ghost of its former self. We switched it off, using its resources for the ship. Later, the other biome residents chose to join the crew, as that was the only sustainable way of going about things."

His words seemed to hold weight, and a vague semblance of truth. Noori nodded, absently, Jai's last words still wrapped around her brain like a dark blanket. She had stopped listening to his voice and had broken the handheld the moment she stepped onto the planet. She wanted to forget him and start things anew. Frankly, she didn't even want to go back to radio. She was being selfish. She thought her voice was meant to calm Jai, only Jai. But it was also unfair. She was stealing someone else's chance at love, at peace, at solace, by being selfish. If it was her voice that was meant to do this, and not anyone else's, then so be it.

"I will try my best, Chief," said Noori.

Pramod smiled and left. Noori sat down in front of the controls and put on the rudimentary headgear that was presented to her. She dialed into the frequency of the Parivartan settlement and began to speak. At first, her words came out all wrong. If she listened to herself, she would balk and break something. So she tried again, and again, and again, until her voice became as tranquil as possible. And then she received her first question, and then the second, and then more, of settlers coming to grips with this strange change, of them missing the stars, of them being too cold, too warm, too lonely, too full, too empty, too human. Noori tried to answer them, best she could. And in all their voices, Noori hoped to find Jai's voice. Every crackle of static gave hope. Every sentence, she imagined, in his voice. And she imagined answering all his pleas. And she imagined the troubles of these people to be Jai's troubles. And she imagined her answers as a balm to Jai's worries. And she imagined their gratitude as Jai's love. And she imagined their escape as her own escape.

She imagined.

ABOUT THE AUTHOR

Amal Singh is an author from Mumbai, India. His short fiction has been longlisted for the BSFA award, and has appeared or is forthcoming in numerous venues such as *Tor.com, Clarkesworld, F&SF, Apex, Asimov's,* among others. His debut novel, *The Garden of Delights* is now out from Flame Tree Press.

The Best Version of Yourself
GRANT COLLIER

Q: What (or who!) is Eudaimon?
A: We are a nonprofit organization that empowers people to live their best lives. A "life," in our view, is best defined simply as a contiguous sequence of experiences, and thus the best life is the one consisting of the best possible experiences.

On a moment-to-moment basis, finding the best experience is actually a well-posed optimization problem, as there are a finite number of possible brain states, and thus a finite number of possible experiences. Some might find this realization limiting: we at Eudaimon find it empowering. Just as the restrictions inherent in the sonnet or the haiku spur poets to new creative heights, this restriction to the set of possible experiences frees us to ask the question—what is the best one? And not only to ask it, but to *answer.*

Our procedure—

Maria stopped reading. The pamphlet wouldn't say anything she hadn't heard before. The wind had carried it, tattered, to her, and she had grabbed it, eager for a distraction from what she was about to do. She stuffed it into her backpack's outer side pocket: old habits.

Still pointing her attention in any direction but one in particular, Maria pondered the now pamphlet-less wind. She liked it: wind, in general. She liked it because it tickled her face, and her hair, and she never knew where it would come from next, and because, after everything, it was still here.

She ought to recycle the pamphlet—was *required* to recycle it. But she was going to compost it. Let Eudaimon mourn the loss of good material that could have become joyjelly.

She continued her walk around the periphery of the pain preserve. She'd made these walks a habit over the past several months, claiming to simply enjoy them—and this grew to be true. Nobody living in the pain preserve would question her reasons for walking so close to the border—being in the preserve themselves, they had all had their own motives for every decision relentlessly questioned, and so shared with each other the courtesy of discretion. And besides, wasn't she technically in charge of maintaining these borders?

No, Maria wasn't worried about her community. Her people: even if they knew what she was doing, they'd all be loyal, but she would never tell them—would never endanger them, out of that same loyalty.

She was, however, worried about Eudaimon's surveillance drones, buzzing obediently around the border: right where the pain preserve ended and the joyjelly began. Any activity out of the ordinary would alert Eudaimon. Maria had needed to make walking on the border—even meandering past it sometimes—seem ordinary for her, like something she did innocently all the time.

Hence the months of regular walks.

Q: Is it possible to be sad while having the best possible sensory experience?
A: Indeed it is; so much of our experience goes beyond the sensory. A person's personality, goals, and memories often play a much larger part in their overall well-being than their immediate phenomenal experiences. However, these can all be represented by some finite arrangement of neurons: we can find the best of each of these, as well!

Q: Is Eudaimon's procedure safe?
A: Our procedure is one hundred percent safe, free of undesired side effects, and fully reversible: however, none of our four million (and growing!) recipients have ever requested the procedure be reversed.

"When I die, I don't want a tombstone," Mom said. They had been waiting for the bus in silence, and nothing in particular had been said to prompt this comment.

"Noted," Maria said. She was unfazed by the spontaneity on display here; that was just Mom. It was fun, in the small doses she got in her visits to town these days.

"And I *don't* want to be cremated."

"I'm not getting you taxidermied," Maria cut in.

Mom continued, seeming not to hear. "I want you to plant a tree above me. But not above my stomach or anything: right above my head, so the roots grow into my brain." She paused suddenly and cracked a delayed smile. "Don't taxidermy me," she said, once Maria's comment had registered.

"I literally just said I wouldn't."

"Good."

"Good."

They sat in contented agreement at this for a second, before Mom reiterated her initial point. "But I want the tree thing. I want to turn into tree roots. So I can feel what it's like."

Maria nodded approvingly. "What kind of tree do you want to eat your brain?"

Mom thought briefly, then waved the question away. "Don't know. Don't remember being any trees, in particular. Can't compare. They're all good, probably." She paused. "Just don't pick a shitty one," she added thoughtfully. The bus emerged from behind a corner, and Mom pointed to it. "Here."

"Why would you remember being a tree?"

"I don't, that's what I said."

The bus pulled to a stop in front of them with a series of hisses and groans whose volume Maria suspected would be mechanically unnecessary if there were sufficient transportation funding. "But why would you *be* a tree?"

"I eat a lot of fruit," said Mom, "so I'm made of fruit, partly. I used to be fruit. But I don't remember that."

The bus doors opened.

"And fruit is trees?"

Mom nodded. "And also, in the future, you know. When you plant one in my brain."

"But not a shitty one," Maria noted.

Mom shook her head solemnly. "Or I'll know."

A small crowd of passengers bustled out of the bus and dispersed. A similarly sized crowd, Maria and Mom among them, bustled inward to take their place. Mid-bustle, a man out-bustled them from behind, pardoning perfunctorily as he passed between them. Seatless, he grabbed a bus pole, turned around, and stared into space. He was grinning euphorically. His appearance and demeanor were not otherwise noteworthy, but this grin seemed out of place. He was staring away, and Maria watched him for a few seconds: the grin did not subside, as if brought on by a particularly grin-worthy passing thought, but instead seemed to have been there all day—this man just grinned euphorically, at a baseline.

His eyes, to Maria, seemed empty.

Mom saw her watching the man and leaned over. "He's a jellyhead. Eudaimon thing. Lot more of them in Manchester." She tapped on her forehead. "Brain's all nanobots."

"I know what a jellyhead is," Maria said pridefully, although truthfully, she'd never seen one in person—people with the money for the treatment didn't tend to live out near where park rangers got stationed. Though wasn't there talk of subsidies now? Had that passed? The man didn't look particularly rich. "And don't talk that loud; he'll hear you."

Mom shrugged. "Doesn't much matter if he does. He can just choose not to be bothered."

Maria continued to stare at the man, until he turned, met her eyes, and waved. Still grinning.

She averted her gaze and did not wave back.

Q: How does Eudaimon's procedure work?

A: Our procedure is built on recent advances in the field of awake brain surgery. This field has exploded in recent years, with the advent of nanobots that can cross the blood-brain barrier. Today, assisted by these devices, surgeons can often perform the procedure without incisions—even remotely—and any removed sections of the brain, along with the nanobots themselves, are dissolved harmlessly into the bloodstream over the next few days.

Eudaimon has repurposed this revolutionary new technology, putting *you* in the driver's seat. There's no need for a surgeon as an intermediary: just think about the way you want to feel, the way you want to be, and the bots will take care of the rest.

Want to stop feeling depressed?

Eudaimon can help.

Want a better work ethic? To be charismatic or confident?

To be more clearheaded or in control of your thoughts?

Eudaimon can help you here, too.

Want to kick your drug addiction?

Eudaimon's treatment can replace the drug effects you crave while curbing all the debilitating symptoms and preserving your ability to function at a high level (if you so wish).

No rehab, no withdrawal, no relapses. Simply concentrate on the way you want to feel, the way you want to be, and our bots will make it so!

Q: How do the nanobots know what changes to make?

A: In short, you tell them! We use a form of machine learning, where the metric the bots optimize for is your own satisfaction. At first, they'll make many small, barely perceptible changes, and sense if you like the results: if not, they'll reverse them, but if so, they'll keep them, and iterate more. Over a few weeks, the traits you want to manifest in yourself will inevitably emerge—and the improvements don't have to stop there!

Maria stood still and checked her GPS: this was where she needed to depart. She remained still.

The edge of Acadia Pain Preserve was abrupt and stark. It was marked by a razor-thin line of lime-green mold, engineered to eat any joyjelly that overstepped its bounds and tried to grow into the preserve itself. Or at least it looked like a line from the surface: it was actually a wall, stretching far down underground, as far as the jelly itself. Straining against the other side of the mold wall was a mass of spongy and reddish soil that seemed to stretch on forever, and perhaps eventually would—but of course, it was not soil anymore, not except for the top protective layer, seeded with just enough engineered lichens not to erode away. If Maria dug here, she would quickly reveal a pink-tan sludge underneath the soil that had settled over it with time—the joyjelly.

The "landscape" still rose and fell in the distance, in a crude imitation of the hills it had replaced—mostly fell, from Maria's relatively high elevation, until farther out it gave way to the ocean. From this edge of the preserve, Maria could see the two "lobes" of Mt. Desert Island. "Like a brain!" her manager had exclaimed excitedly when orienting her to the job years ago, not yet realizing how deeply, darkly funny that observation would become.

Farther still was the mainland, where the joyjelly resumed and continued farther than Maria could see, with few interruptions. Both island-side and mainland-side, the jelly was dotted with meter-long identical solar panels, every few meters or so. They looked jarringly artificial, particularly next to the heavily-forested preserve. As if the world hadn't fully rendered past the point where Maria was standing. The sun was rising behind her, and their long shadows eclipsed each other geometrically.

Maria released the breath she hadn't realized she'd been holding and stepped forward onto the joyjelly, gingerly. It squished subtly under the soil as if it might give way, though it didn't—Eudaimon built for the long-term. Maria checked her GPS again: about a thirty-mile journey from here, one-way.

Eudaimon's drones hovered, curious, nearby. She heard their faint buzzing under the wind but resisted the urge to look, even out of the corner of her eye: if she looked, they would look back and see her looking. What legitimate reason could she have for looking? She had to assume they would let her be, if ignored.

Truthfully, they probably would. Tensions between the preserves and Eudaimon had died down over the past few years. Certainly not out of a lack of resentment—rather, because rage can only burn so long while impotent, and in more of Maria's fellow residents every year, it had burned into begrudging complacency or inert depression. Both of these outcomes were acceptable to Eudaimon, as they led to no hostile action—and the latter made their treatment more attractive. These minimal security measures were a "gesture of goodwill," according to Em, who seemed sure that all Eudaimon needed to win, in the long-term, was to wait—but the less mental energy Maria devoted to Em, the better. All that was important about Em was that she was wrong: because Maria was not complacent, and she was not—inert, at least.

Maria still had all her rage left.

She walked onward.

Q: What is Nirvana?
A: Nirvana is the particular state toward which the brains of all Eudaimon's satisfied beneficiaries seem to eventually evolve. Even brains that began extremely differently will tend to, of their own accord, make themselves into this very particular set of neural connections.

We can think of any physical system—a category that includes brains—as existing at some point on a spectrum of well-being, at a given point in time. Some physical systems are happy: others are sad, others neutral. Others still, it is theorized, have no feelings at all, although this has never been proven. We use gradient ascent on this spectrum of well-being: this is a fancy way of saying that we find where your brain is on this spectrum, and nudge it, bit by bit, until it's happier. If we do this enough, then as sure as a ball will roll to the center of a funnel, your brain will converge to the happiest possible physical system: that's what Nirvana is.

Q: Is it true that people in Nirvana are paralyzed?
A: While it is true that brains in Nirvana are no longer attached to bodily nerve endings, it is not true that they cannot move. They are able to reattach those nerve endings at any time they wish, but simply

choose not to, having found a much better use for them. Exactly what that use entails can only be fully understood through introspection, by those in Nirvana themselves.

Note that those who have undergone our treatment, having inevitably developed into very pragmatically minded people at this advanced stage, will take efforts to ensure they will be able to receive all the nutrients they need to function, on a biological level, before ascending into Nirvana.

While several nutrient-distribution solutions are already on the market, these are often unreliable and will require some level of continual outside intervention by those who are un-ascended. Eudaimon, however, is currently developing a cost-effective device that will serve all the needs of those wishing to ascend into Nirvana. We plan to produce this device at scale in the coming years.

Mom loved the idea of rugged outdoorswomanship, but only the idea. She claimed to be, in her heart, a spirit of the forest, but truthfully was much too dependent on the comforts of the city to act much like it. Maria had indulged her and taken her camping in the park once—half a time, really—before she decided it didn't matter how refreshing the forest air was: hotel rooms had fewer bugs.

Maria blamed herself a bit for this—she was going to rent a cabin, had it planned, with the tab pulled up, but she'd waited too long to make the actual reservation, and so convinced Mom to camp dispersed instead; that was too woodsy too fast, it was no wonder Mom couldn't tough it.

They made the most of it, though—both hotel beds, pushed together, made a base just large enough to support the tent, and they built it right there in the hotel. Room service had S'mores-flavored ice cream, and they turned out the lights and turned on "Ambient Nature Sounds Free 10 Hrs. No Ads (High Quality!)," and it was kind of like the real thing.

"I think you might be my best friend," Mom said in the bed-tent, once the festivities had died down and the night had reached the point where it was late and still enough to say things that were really true. "I don't think it's supposed to be like that. I know I'm not yours."

Maria didn't know what to say to this. "I like spending time with you, Mom."

"I just can't seem to keep any friends," Mom continued, seeming satisfied enough with this answer. "At least not any I didn't give birth to. I push them away. I don't commit. I forget to." She was silent for a while. "I think maybe I should try getting treated for my ADHD again."

Maria was relieved to hear this: a relief born from years of resignation suddenly reversed. "Yeah? That's honestly great, Mom. You could try my meds if you want; we're about the same weight."

There was the rustle of Mom's head shaking in the dark. "I know it works for you, but I just never felt like myself. Side effects." She shuddered. A short silence turned into a long one. "I've actually—I've been thinking about maybe trying Eudaimon."

Maria felt a fear then—a small, passing fear, but one that was small only because it was so distant. If she thought any more about it, examined it up close, then it was a fear so great and large that it had to be irrational, could not be addressed fully as anything else, and thus could only be dismissed. "Eudaimon bots treat a lot more than just ADHD, Mom. You sure you want something that invasive?"

"It's only as invasive as I want it to be," Mom said. "If I make any other changes, and I don't like them, I can just switch it back." She paused. "I'm just so *tired* sometimes. I want a break from . . . from being myself." She sighed. "Or maybe I don't want to change who I am—I just want to be a better version of me. Maybe that's what all these treatments are getting at. I think Eudaimon might help me be the best version of me."

Maria held her mother's hand then. "I'm honestly really proud of you for thinking about this stuff Mom. And I'll support whatever you decide."

Mom's hand squeezed back.

Maria fell asleep soon after. She woke up once in the middle of that night. Groggy and unremembering, she looked at the dead still tent fabric above her head, and thought it odd that there was no wind.

Q: Is ascending into Nirvana reversible?

A: Initial ascension is a fully reversible process—but not one that, to our knowledge, has been voluntarily reversed. We have experimented briefly with reversing it forcibly with rats but ran up against ethical concerns when the subjects expressed great distress: it seems that once Nirvana has been experienced, any return to a more traditional baseline brain state feels torturous. We've attempted to work around this issue by first inducing selective amnesia: purging any prior memories of Nirvana, so that there is nothing to be "missed." Unfortunately, the very experience of having these memories purged appears to be equivalently distressing to the subjects. Because of this, Eudaimon considers it an ethical imperative not to perform reversal procedures on any physical system in Nirvana.

Q: What is Nirvana X?

A: Nirvana X is our most cutting-edge program yet. Its purpose is twofold:

- To increase the space- and energy-efficiency of our Nirvana-holding facilities.
- To meet what we see as the ethical imperative to allow as much of the world as possible to escape non-Nirvana.

The recent demand for our products has been so great that, even with the support of an international coalition of governments, our current production capabilities require us to find a more efficient way of processing Nirvana-sustaining units. The bottleneck here, surprisingly, is no longer the production of nanobots, or the administration of the procedure itself, but the energy consumption of sustaining a whole human body autonomously once the nerve endings have retracted.

Nirvana X is an elegant solution to this: as it turns out, keeping the entire human body intact and operational is a very inefficient way of powering the brain. What's more, the raw material present in such a body can be repurposed and used to make many more Nirvana states than just the one, evolved out of someone's original brain: with current methods, usually around ten brain-sized units total, per body: hence the moniker "X." These new "brains" are essentially physically indistinguishable from more naturally evolved Nirvana brains, and thus we have every reason to believe they are experiencing just as much bliss. This entire array of joyous beings can be sustained at a fraction of the energy cost of a single human body in ordinary Nirvana. We see Nirvana X as the future of what we have to offer.

Crossing the joyjelly, Maria tried not to look at her footprints. The topsoil was thin here, and so any indentations—footprints included—filled immediately with red fluid, pumping up from below. Not quite blood: not anymore. It had mixed with the elements, taken on enough that to call it "blood" was too simplistic, though to call it anything else seemed even more of a lie.

The not-blood was part of the water cycle now. When it got hot enough, it evaporated, and so some days the rain was red. Maria glanced upward at the thought, but the sky remained considerably cloudless, for now.

Maria was nearing the shoreline and spotted the causeway that connected it to the mainland: one of the few things in sight not built to sustain joyjelly. She angled herself toward it and took stock of her situation: she was making good time. Better than the first hour or so, when she hadn't yet learned to ignore the rhythmic squish of her steps. But then, the squish itself had lessened as she'd approached closer to the shore. The layer of mud covering the jelly at lower elevations was thicker—no doubt to Eudaimon's dismay; any non-jelly material was a waste in their eyes, though luckily, they had not yet learned to conquer entropy. It squished more like mud, and less like a brain: if not for the field of solar panels, and the bloody footprints behind her, Maria might have briefly forgotten what she was walking on. The drones were nowhere to be seen—they must have decided to pay her no mind. Her backpack felt heavy, but not overly so: unexpectedly light, in fact, given everything in it.

Maria didn't need such a large backpack: much of it was superfluous junk, packed to look as confusing as possible to a drone's X-rays, though this was done more out of superstition than any proof of efficacy. She'd used the junk, also, as a layer separating the topmost, clearly innocent items—food, water, bags of both the sleeping- and wag- variety—from the more suspect ones. The most clearly illicit item was packed into the very bottom: a large clump of pale green joyjelly neutralizing mold, curated from months of scraping the bottoms of her shoes after deliberately smudging them on the perimeter of the preserve.

Maria remembered the first time it had rained red. Em had apologized profusely at the ensuing preserve meeting, assuring that they were working on a solution.

"Em" was the name of Eudaimon's ambassador to Acadia Pain Preserve—though it was also the name of every other ambassador. She was alarmingly gorgeous—most mid- to late-stage jellyheads were, having complete control of their endocrine and metabolic systems. Charismatic, too. It helped them to manipulate you, convince you to be like them, run for office, run the world, destroy the world. Until they did away with their bodies entirely, and suddenly became indistinguishable from everyone else currently squishing under Maria's feet.

By around the eighth time it rained red, Em's apologies stopped. The implication was simple: Eudaimon already had a solution in mind. *The red rain doesn't bother the joyjelly. Wouldn't you love it if it didn't bother you either?*

It was considered a great sacrifice, staying behind as an ambassador, in a real body—most could only manage it for a couple of years before the call to "ascension" became too strong. Em did it out of the goodness of her heart, she claimed. She stayed behind, at great emotional cost to herself, just to help guide poor, unmodified souls like Maria out of their suffering. She'd been the ambassador to this preserve almost since the beginning—back when it was still a National Park, saved from jellyhood by a quirk of the legal system, and collecting unmodified squatters as a result. Almost fifteen years now: a real commitment to the cause.

Maria hated Em. Em seemed to regard Maria with the same cheerful, detached benevolence she regarded most everything with—this made Maria hate her more. Ostensibly, they ought to work closely together, as Maria was the senior-most park official left, but Maria tended to avoid associating with her as much as possible—her job was to keep Eudaimon *out* of their community's affairs, not help them ingratiate themselves more. As far as she was concerned, they had very little to talk about.

At the shoreline, the jelly sank underneath the water, while the panels stayed floating on top, tethered by increasingly long cables to the ocean floor. This was broken only by the causeway, ancient seeming in the context of its surroundings: a low bridge, made of stone and steel and concrete, predating anything Eudaimon built. As Maria stepped onto it, it didn't remotely squish.

It was midday now, and she sat down on the causeway, stopping for lunch. It was the most scenic stop she was going to get after leaving Acadia: the water surrounded her on both sides, lapped gently at the sides of the causeway, and helped her forget about what was lurking underneath. There was even some green out here: molds and natural lichens that had taken hold on the top layer of soil, or on the solar panels. Eudaimon evidently didn't patrol these areas, miles from the preserve, at least not well enough to keep some semblance of life from taking back over. That boded well for Maria; she hoped this trend continued farther out. She removed her lunch from the top backpack layer. Most of the preserves' food was shipped in from material-efficient vertical farms, but all of this—apart from some nutrient bars—was grown on-site. The trees it grew from now were newer—genetically modified to handle the higher iron content oozing in from the surrounding joyjelly—but Maria preferred not to think about that.

She ate. She then packed her waste into her bag—*leave no trace*, she thought, snorting—and moved on.

At the end of the causeway was the mainland, where the joyjelly and solar panels continued, seemingly identical to those on the side Maria had come from. But not completely identical, Maria noticed with excitement when she began walking past them; there was a key difference. The smooth, simple stones that served as the backs of the solar panels were not fully blank on this side of the causeway: rather, each held a simple, small engraving. "*Casey Berger*," read the one to

Maria's left. *"John Kevin Rogers,"* read the next one as she passed. Then *"Laramie Graber." "Allegra Gulino." "Dina Rubina."*

The solar panels doubled as gravestones. Eudaimon was efficient as always.

The joyjelly on the island, near the preserve, hadn't been made of people—at least, not anything that had been a person directly before being jelly. They wouldn't put that jelly so close to unmodifieds—at least not people with known names. It was intimidating. Bad for recruitment. That jelly was made from trees and grass and air and water and dirt. The remains of actual people—they were farther out. Still closer to the vestiges of civilization than most, but far enough out that they couldn't be seen unless sought out.

Maria allowed herself a grim smile. She had made it to the named jelly. She was getting closer.

Q: Do people have a free choice to ascend into Nirvana? Do they still have free will?

A: Contrary to some popular myths, a deep respect for individual autonomy is one of Eudaimon's core values: as evidenced in no small part by our extensive preservation efforts. We take significant steps to ensure that our technology is only ever used responsibly, with this core value in mind. That being said, it is possible—and happens frequently—that someone becomes who they want to be, only to discover that this new person they've become does not want to be themselves. An initial revulsion at the idea of Nirvana may naturally disappear as a side effect of other changes someone induces within themselves: a sense of open-mindedness, a calming of anxieties, a commitment to rational thought. This may happen multiple times in succession, with each version of themselves wishing to become something new, until the end destination is something that the individual, pre-modification, would have never explicitly claimed to have wanted. It is, however, what we all seem to want—and freely choose—in the end.

Q: Do non-brains, other organisms, or nonliving matter entering Nirvana freely choose to do so?

A: This is an astute question, as it acknowledges the fact—commonly denied—that no physical system is categorically distinct from any other. In fact, insofar as a "will" is a term for the true desires and intentions of a brain, there is an analogous quantity for all types of matter. When developing the technology for ascending non-brains into Nirvana, we didn't begin from purely mechanical principles: we instead developed nanobots capable of, as far as we can verify, deciphering the intentions of non-brains regarding themselves, and making those intentions come to pass.

Maria saw her mother dissolve in real time. It took three, maybe four months. Faster than most.

You know your lifelong dream of hiking the Appalachian Trail? Mom texted her, a couple of weeks after the treatment.

Yeah lol. What about it? Maria replied.

Let's do it.

Maria felt giddy at the thought. She had even been thinking about going soon, but the excuses not to go yet—work, season's not perfect to start, she should train more first—were exactly sufficient to have dissuaded her. Truthfully, the excuses were always exactly sufficient, by a razor-thin margin, seemingly cropping up in precisely the right number and magnitude to prevent any actual action. *Mom, you don't even like hiking.*

I like it now.

On video, Mom hadn't looked any different after the treatment, but Maria didn't actually see her in person until they met at the trailhead, a few weeks later.

It was late morning when Maria walked up to find Mom already there. She didn't look different in person, either, at first. They had planned to meet in the early morning: Maria had, as was custom, aimed to purposely arrive an hour late so as to only have to wait an hour or so for Mom to arrive. As was also custom, she'd unintentionally added a half hour or so of lateness on top of this, all on her own.

Mom was smiling when they met—Maria had expected her to be smiling like the subway man, widely, vacantly, but she wasn't. Just smiling: a subdued smile, a half-smile really, with a scrunching around her eyes, like she knew some private joke that Maria could not understand. She carried a backpack that Maria had never seen before, seemingly bought for the trip. Maria apologized for her lateness, newly self-conscious, and Mom waved it away, stepping forward to hug her—"I know how it is." The hug smelled the same as it always had—she hadn't expected the bots to have a scent: or maybe she had. "You ready?" Mom asked.

"Am *I* ready?" Maria laughed. "Are *you* ready? I'm reminding you again—nobody of your experience level should be doing this. It's honestly *dangerous*. And tiring. I'm fully expecting to have to drop you back into civilization before we reach Virginia. At the latest. You might not make it to North Carolina."

"It can't be that bad," Mom said. "And besides, I have my daughter here with me, if anything goes wrong."

"You're insane," Maria said. She told herself it was only a joke.

"Maybe," Mom said, and tousled Maria's hair, and flashed a full smile, with perhaps just a hint of the subway-man showing, but it could have been imagined.

The trail was beautiful. It was arduous, and tedious, and strenuous, and insufficiently populated with fresh food, restrooms, or basic sanitation products, and absolutely beautiful.

They hiked in silence, mostly. Maria had been worried Mom would want to talk, being the more extroverted between them. Mom seemed to understand this and gave Maria the silence she needed. She'd sometimes hang back until she was out of sight, but just barely, for hours at a time. Not because she couldn't keep pace with Maria—she was surprisingly resilient. Maria suspected she was being courteous. The hanging-back always seemed to happen right before an overlook, so Maria could spend the first few minutes by herself, on top of the world.

It was less beautiful at night. They packed separate tents, so at the end of each day, they would pitch them, and retreat, exhausted, inside. Maria would normally fall asleep near-instantaneously. Still, she often woke to the sound of laughing.

Mom laughed in her sleep. Hysterically, sometimes even painfully, it sounded.

She would wake up smiling bemusedly as if nothing odd had occurred.

"Do you remember anything about last night?" Maria asked, after the first night.

"Not to brag, but I remember everything now." They had been dancing around talking about the procedure, and this was the closest either of them had gotten to mentioning it explicitly. It caught Maria off guard. "At least, I remember everything I remember." A quick widening of her smile that ducked away as soon as it appeared, like it was hiding. "What's on your mind?"

"Did you dream anything? In your sleep . . . you made some sounds."

"I feel like my dreams felt . . . peaceful. I woke up very happy." Smiling. Reminiscing. "I don't remember any specifics though, no."

Maria didn't mention it again.

Midday that day, they stopped at the edge of a clearing, in a position so as to admire the sunlit view but not become too sunlit themselves.

Maria unfastened her pack and retrieved a package of mush advertising itself as adventurous and full of all the essential nutrients she needed to conquer any challenge. It had a picture of a man standing on top of a mountain, and also a dog. It tasted, purportedly, like Mountain Blast. Mom retrieved the same, though hers was Hiker Fuel flavored. She then told Maria to close her eyes, shuffled through her pack again, and placed a plastic bag of something into Maria's hands.

Maria opened her eyes and laughed. "What the fuck Mom—"

"Surprise!" Mom's hands became briefly infused with jazz.

"—we're supposed to pack *light*," Maria said. "What is this, forty grams? Where did you even get this?"

"It's my stash," Mom said. "I figured you could put it to good use. I was saving it for a special occasion, but there's the overlook today, I thought we could watch the sunset with it."

"This is years' worth. This will last us years."

"You, not us." Mom smiled faintly. "I don't need it anymore."

The sun set too fast. It would never come back, just dark forever, and it would never come back, it was too late, they took it, and it would never come back, no matter what she did. She shook and cried in a ball, and Mom held her patiently, for hours, until she calmed down.

"Just like old times," she said to Maria the next day. "You used to have the worst dreams, you know."

Things were easier afterward. Maria had been scared to talk to her; scared she wasn't really her mother anymore. But she still was.

"Do you feel like your ADHD is gone?"

Mom thought for a moment. "Not gone. Covered up, maybe. You know I joined a backpacking group?"

"I know, you're an expert at this now." Maria's voice betrayed some real annoyance.

"A lot of people get new hobbies after the procedure, I think. Most of my group has had it done. Some have even hiked this trail before." It felt like a subtle prod, to test if Maria had fully accepted her decision, or perhaps to gain that acceptance.

"That's great for them," Maria said.

"I'm forgetting things less too," Mom said. "And I have more energy now. You know my desk, by the fridge? It's a real desk now. Cleared out. I'd had a picture of you on it, hiding behind all the clutter. I can see it now, every day."

• • •

Maria had forgotten to pack a rain cover. The first night it rained, it did so torrentially, and she woke in the middle of the night to find her tent flooding. She hurriedly half-disassembled her tent and rushed it, still billowing with air, into Mom's. Mom bolted upright and helped her tumble inside and bring in the rest of her belongings. She zipped the flap closed behind her—caught it on the tent, unzipped, pulled it in, re-zipped—and they both sat there for a moment, breathless, staring at each other.

Mom laughed.

Maria laughed too, and then Mom laughed harder. This continued for several minutes, with several cycles in which they would nearly regain composure, but then start up again. This was sometimes triggered by a glance at Maria's tent piled inside, poles sticking out and waterlogged like some misplaced sea creature, or more often by a glance at each other, lips twitching upward involuntarily.

The laughing settled down eventually: Maria retrieved her supplies from within the fully soaked tent and pushed its remains back outside. She would sleep in Mom's tent that night.

Maria didn't need a sleeping bag to sleep, but Mom insisted on lending her own, that it would make a greater difference to Maria's comfort than to hers. "I really don't mind."

Maria accepted gratefully. "I still can't believe you were the one more prepared for this trip," she said. "I'm the literal ranger. I've camped maybe hundreds of times, and still—"

"Excuse me, that's my daughter you're talking about," Mom said. "You'll treat her with respect." After a pause: " . . . anyway, we both know I'm cheating. So it's not a fair comparison."

Maria laughed. "Thanks." After a reciprocal pause: "I'm cheating too, you know. Been cheating, actually, for much longer. Or, you know. Should be."

"You're not taking anything right now?" Mom asked.

"Should be," Maria repeated. "But I don't need it so much out here." She gestured outward, past the thin tent fabric that was currently stretched over her, shivering violently in the wind, even under the rain cover. "Keeps my head clear. It's simple, and it's physical, and it . . . makes sense. There's no schedules and no responsibilities."

"So you don't take it?" Mom asked.

"Sometimes. When I can. Just to prove I don't need it. That I'm not . . . dependent, I guess. Out here, I like to be myself all the way. Where it can't hurt anyone."

"You still forget rain covers though," Mom noted.

"Yeah, well, I wasn't out here yet when I was packing," Maria laughed. "And also, you're cheating more."

Mom laughed back. "Fair."

They cuddled in the now-damp tent for warmth that night. Maria laughed no more, after saying goodnight, but Mom, lying exposed on the damp floor of her tent, continued laughing all through the night.

"Mom, you're bleeding."

There was blood streaming from both of Mom's ankles, in the spots where her tall hiking shoes rubbed with every step. Her thick socks came to just under each wound and had filled with blood all around the rim. Mom looked down casually. "So I am."

"How could you . . . " Maria swung her backpack down, kneeled on the muddy path, and rummaged efficiently for the first aid kit. "How did this happen?"

"Now that you mention it," Mom said, still staring idly at her blood-soaked socks, "they'd been chafing for a while. Think my boots don't fit right."

"Why didn't you *say* anything?" Maria unsheathed an alcohol swab and gestured that a foot ought to be placed in her hand.

Mom sat down cross-legged in the mud and extended the top foot outward. "I really don't mind, you know. It doesn't hurt."

"There's no pain?" Maria inspected the wound: it looked as though it had been inflicted repeatedly, for a while now.

Not just today.

Mom smiled pensively as Maria set the alcohol swab against her open wound. No wincing, no discomfort. "There's pain," she explained. "But pain doesn't hurt. Not if I don't want."

Maria studied her mother's face. She held the alcohol swab over the wound—longer than was medically necessary. Mom's face held no reaction. Maria continued to press the swab into her ankle. She squeezed it, so more of the alcohol came out, drizzled in. Was she squeezing her ankle too hard? She was really pressing it in, staring at Mom's face all the while. She wanted to see *something* there, some discomfort, anything.

Mom smiled calmly back.

Eventually, Maria broke eye contact and reached for the gauze. "Still. You could get infected. Pay attention to the pain. You're gonna want to keep your ankles." Maria made eye contact again, and this time Mom looked away.

"Of course," she said.

Maria wished she had met her eyes, but didn't want to analyze this thought too much. She cleaned the other ankle, then taped the gauze to the affected areas of both. "You should be set for now," she said. "But just—in the future, can you pretend that pain bothers you? And *tell me*, if you feel it?"

"Of course." Another smile, but this one seemed perhaps tinged with sadness.

There was an aspen grove. It was early fall when they came to it, and the yellow and white stretched on for as far as they could see. This was about three-quarters of the way through the trail; they'd been making good time and would reach the end before winter hit.

Maria looked back to ensure Mom was following and saw her smiling widely, perhaps too widely. Perhaps admiring the grove, she thought, but this was not the first time this had happened, and it unnerved her. Maria herself had been smiling but stopped. She waited for Mom to catch up. "Enjoying the scenery?"

"Oh, yes," Mom said and flashed Maria a smile smaller than the one she'd been wearing before.

"They're all one tree, you know," Maria said. "Connected by the roots." Maria knew she used trivia to distract herself from her feelings—she thought this even as she said it.

"Different, but the same," Mom said. "Interconnected." She seemed to love the idea.

Maria nodded. "One aspen could be a whole forest."

Mom smiled appreciatively and stood in place for a while, admiring it.

Maria stood beside her. She opened her mouth tentatively. "When you smile—" she said, but stopped herself, as she didn't know how to phrase it.

Mom stared at her, expecting.

Maria spoke quickly then—the words tumbled out of her. "You smile wider when you don't think I'm looking."

Mom's face was carefully neutral now. Diplomatic. "Would you prefer I smile wider when we're talking?"

"No, I . . . it just feels, sometimes, like you're hiding it from me. Like you don't want to upset me."

Another light smile this time, tinged with sadness—jellyheads shouldn't ever be sad, should they? *Unless they want to be*, Maria thought. "I don't," Mom said. "I thought you wouldn't want to be upset, either. Do you want—"

"I want you to act how you feel," Maria said. It came out more harshly than she had expected, but perhaps no more harshly than she intended.

Mom sighed.

"Did you feel that sigh? Was that sigh really you?" Maria asked.

"No." She sighed again.

"Why are you *hiding*?" Maria asked. "Stop hiding from me. Be *yourself*. Be who you really are. Don't try to relate to me. I want to know what you're really like, right now."

Mom's face became neutral again, then suddenly expanded into a sickening smile.

Maria's world changed. Her deepest fears and anxieties about her mother, about the world, were no longer that: from this point onward, they were simply beliefs.

Maria settled her face into the neutral expression that Mom had been wearing a moment prior. It looked remarkably similar because their mouths and eyes untwisted in the same way, and it was remarkably easy because she was fully numb. "Thanks for your honesty." She turned away and began walking again. They should be able to make ten more miles before sundown and setting up camp. If she walked them quickly enough, she could stay numb.

"I didn't want to make you sad," Mom said. Maria didn't turn back, kept walking, but she knew the smile was still there: she heard it in her voice. "I want you to be happy," she continued.

Maria plowed forward, unresponsive.

Mom ran ahead of her and turned around. She'd un-smiled now: re-pretending. "Maria, please," she said. "I just wanted to be honest. I just wanted to make you happy."

Maria walked past her and did not make eye contact. Who was there to make eye contact with? Maria was the only person left in these woods.

"I thought you'd want me to be happy, too," Mom said.

"I want you to be *you*." She'd meant to contain her anger here, speak neutrally, but it exploded out of her now. "I want my *mother* back."

"I am me," Mom said. "I'm a better version of myself now—Maria, you can't understand it if you haven't felt it." Mom's tone was placating, as if Maria were complaining that she had to finish her vegetables before digging for worms outside. *You'll understand when you're older.*

Maria stopped where Mom blocked her path. "Why are you hiking this trail?"

"I wanted to do something with you," Mom said. She seemed to stop her sentence early: Maria didn't know which words had been omitted but sensed the first unspoken word was *before.*

"For you, or for me?" Maria asked. She had another question, also unspoken: *what happens when this is over?*

"Why can't I just want my daughter to be happy?" Mom asked. "Is that so wrong? Maria—you just can't understand what it's like." Dodging the spoken question—but perhaps answering the unspoken.

"You're right," Maria said. "I don't understand." She pushed past Mom again, walking quickly. Her lower jaw was shaking involuntarily, and she knew Mom saw it, and knew Mom knew it meant she was going to cry from anger, Maria hated that she angry-cried, but Mom angry-cried too, except not anymore, she could probably cry or not cry whenever she wanted now, and it didn't mean anything either way. At this thought, the surface tension in Maria's eyes broke, and she had to run so Mom couldn't see, and also running helped her not to scream.

Maria knew she couldn't outrun Mom: she cared if her legs hurt, and Mom didn't. She stopped right before what she thought was the overlook because she didn't want to see this one alone, they were supposed to do it together, they were supposed to be together, Mom was supposed to actually *be here* with her, but she had betrayed her, and now she wasn't anywhere anymore. Maria sat against a tree and began methodically picking apart one of its fallen branches, trying to catch her breath. Mom caught up to her there. "It's really helped me," she offered immediately, not stopping to catch her breath. "You know that."

"You didn't need that much help," Maria said. "I wanted to support you, but you could have tried something else first."

" . . . But I know now there's so much more, too," Mom continued. "I can feel it."

"There's *so much* you could have tried *first*," Maria said. "You think I haven't struggled with the same issues as you? It's just ADHD. Jesus Mom, you didn't take any meds at all, for *decades,* then you skipped right to *nanobots* in your *fucking brain.*"

"Maria, you don't understand what it's like," Mom repeated. "I know you must be scared for me, but it's not scary, it's exciting."

"You didn't even really try to work on yourself," Maria said. "Because that—"

"Maria—"

"No, listen. Because that would take *effort.* You'd have to actually *work* at it. Like *I* have. I've worked hard enough, I don't even *need* meds half the time, and you didn't even show me how to do that, I had to learn it myself. But you took the easy fix. You *always* do. And you thought it wouldn't go the way it would for other people who do it because you don't think ahead that far."

"I didn't—"

"But now you're telling me you don't even want to exist as yourself at all anymore. And honestly, that's the worst outcome. It'd be better if you'd just stayed broken."

"I know that you—"

Maria covered her face with her hands and screamed until her breath ran out, then inhaled and screamed again. Finally, she uncovered her face and stared dead ahead, with eyes too blurred to face anything in particular, not caring to wipe them.

"I understand you're hurt," Mom said, speaking carefully. "And I also understand that there's no way for me to make that hurt go away and that you'll never understand what I'm feeling without getting the treatment yourself." She paused, as if to consider applying pressure in this direction, but declined to do so. "But Maria—I can feel myself moving toward a peace I've never known, that I didn't even know was possible. It's so much bigger than me as a person, or you, or any of us, and I can join with it and be a part of it." Mom was smiling.

"You know the one thing Eudaimon couldn't fix about you?" Maria said hoarsely. "That you wanted to get their treatment in the first place. Instead of just living your life. You ran scared, and now all the bots in your brain will tell you that's the right decision, and they'll never let you see how fucked up it was."

Mom was silent.

"How long have you wanted this?" Maria asked. "Since the beginning of the trip?"

"Before," Mom said. "I wanted to be with you . . . " she trailed off and left the words *one last time* unsaid but not unheard.

"And you probably wanted to convince me," Maria said. "To join you."

"You don't seem convincible," Mom said. "But know you don't have to keep suffering like this. I hope you know that."

"You're probably going out as soon as the trip ends, then. You're leaving me. Forever."

"It doesn't have to be forever."

Maria attempted to stare into her mother's eyes then but could only manage to stare *at* them. She couldn't see into them: there was simply a gentle smile and a wall behind which she felt she would never reach.

The trip ended abruptly. The Appalachian Trail didn't exist anymore: not all of it. Right at the border between Maryland and Pennsylvania, it ended. A sea of joyjelly cut through the woods: to the west, it was being built farther out, and to the east, it covered the mountains and continued for farther than Maria could see. Maria had planned ahead based on older references, ones she had compiled years ago and not thought to update. It dawned on her that they had been meeting very few people on the trail the past few days.

They didn't speak much, when they came to it: hadn't spoken much at all, since their conversation in the aspen grove. They hadn't really been walking together anymore: only walking alone in the same place.

Independently, they decided to walk up as close to the joyjelly line as possible. It was fresh here, exposed. Maria toed the line carefully, fighting back a revulsion. Mom carefully walked out onto it, then seemed to half-dance; revel in it, as if it were the most beautiful scenery they had come across in the whole trip. Her ankles were bleeding again, and Maria saw a few drops shake off into the jelly. *She's already joining them,* Maria thought.

Mom glanced back at her and smiled.

Q: A friend or family member of mine has joined with others in Nirvana—can I still see or communicate with them?

A: Every person who fully enters Nirvana does so with the understanding that they will likely never revert to their pre-Nirvana state. However, every part of a contiguous Nirvana mass is neuronally interconnected with every other part, and signals travel between these parts frequently: those of us outside of such a mass, of course, have no way of interpreting these signals, but we have every reason to believe they serve the purposes and desires of those within the mass. Given this, and given that Nirvana treatments are offered free of charge to any willing candidate, communicating with a loved one is easy, though, of course, the treatment allowing for such a thing may take several years to fully take effect.

Doing this, of course, will prevent any communication with other loved ones outside of the Nirvana mass of your choosing. Eudaimon's plans to mitigate this are twofold: firstly, any loved ones who have not undergone our treatment may simply do so and join whichever mass you are a part of in order to keep in contact with you. Secondly, any loved ones currently residing as part of a Nirvana mass noncontiguous with your own will soon be reunited, as part of our ongoing efforts at network expansion.

Q: What if I refuse Eudaimon's treatment?

A: Individuals who refuse our treatment are, of course, free to do so. This is not simply an ethical commitment of Eudaimon—though it is that—it is also a mechanical fact of our treatment itself. A handful of outlier cases in which an unwilling individual has been mistakenly treated show that our treatment has the capability to self-cannibalize if unwanted. This is expected: our treatment's main purpose is to manifest its hosts' intentions regarding themselves into reality, and if those intentions are set on not ascending whatsoever, then the treatment will recognize such a thing. Of course, oftentimes an individual has multiple conflicting intentions, and these will tend to work themselves out into a thermal equilibrium until they all align; this means that some individuals, who in the past have outwardly expressed a disinterest in Nirvana, have been known to evolve into it anyway, based on some seed of internal conflict with their stated intentions.

Still, there do exist individuals who genuinely have no current desire to enter Nirvana whatsoever. Provisional living quarters for such individuals, preserved as un-encroachable by the Nirvana networks, are in the works. Some of these provisions include memorials for those who such individuals care about, but who have themselves joined the network. While not communication, these memorials will hopefully allow for some semblance of peace.

Quaking aspen saplings needed a few key elements to grow.

They should be planted in early spring: around now, in fact.

They needed sunlight (in ample supply here), and they needed to be watered regularly, in a quantity-per-watering roughly similar to that which Maria carried in her backpack's second water pouch.

They needed about fifteen inches of soil or compost: the layer of soil that had collected on top of the joyjelly reached ten inches here. Ideally, they would have rich soil all the way down: joyjelly was fattier than Maria would prefer but would make adequate compost at the bottom, particularly if treated with some of the lichens Maria had mixed with the lime-green mold. That was the point of this whole endeavor anyway: she didn't just want to plant the sapling anywhere. She wanted to plant it in—

There was no need to dwell on it before she arrived.

The sun was setting, and the solar-tombstones' shadows were long once again, from the other side. They overlapped, partially obscuring engraved coordinates, writ smaller than the names on each tombstone. Pairs of numbers, the first of which matched the first coordinate Maria had memorized, and the second of which ticked down toward the second—the number she was now repeating under her breath. She was almost here; if she looked up, she could probably see it now but wouldn't be able to discern it from the others until she saw the name.

At this thought, she did look up—she wanted to see it, even if she didn't know which "it" it was—and saw . . . something. A figure, black against the encroaching dusk. Leaning against a tombstone, about a hundred meters off.

Maria was not alone.

She thought that she ought to duck down but knew this was ridiculous: she had been visible for a while, and the figure seemed to be facing her. It was, in fact, standing about where her destination should be.

Maria continued walking. Of course she did. What else could she do?

Slowly now, tentatively, but she had nowhere else to go, and she would not turn back. Perhaps walking slowly would give her time to think of escape routes she knew did not exist. Maybe she would look casual: "I'm just out here, taking a stroll. Just strolling, all day, in a straight line, miles from the preserve, in the most suspicious possible direction."

The details of the figure filled in as Maria approached.

It was Em. Of course it was Em. Who else would it be?

Her posture was relaxed, patient. Her face was blankly cheery. Her eyes were fixed on Maria, and once Maria was a few meters away, she waved.

Maria didn't respond. She instead glanced at the tombstone Em was leaning against—her hand covered part of the name, but she followed Maria's gaze and moved it away, courteous.

It was Mom. Of course it was Mom. Who else would it be?

They both stood for a moment, staring at each other. Em was clearly declining to speak first—if Maria declined as well, then, the conversation never needed to happen. Maybe Em just wanted to watch. Maria set her pack next to Mom's tombstone and began unloading her supplies. She'd need to move the panel before she could begin digging. She fetched the shovel, sticking out of the pack as the tallest item she'd brought. Em was eyeing her pleasantly, curiously, as if she were a zoo animal that had escaped its cage but wasn't particularly dangerous and had nowhere to go, besides. It was only when she touched the shovel to the base of her mother's grave, dug in like a crowbar, that Em spoke up.

"Do you think I'll let you do that?"

It wasn't a threat—or rather, it wasn't only that. Em's very presence here was a threat, of course: she was physically stronger than Maria and backed up by the most powerful organization in the world—the only powerful organization left in the world. She had no visible weapons, but had she pressed a gun to Maria's head, the situation would not have changed. Yet she managed to make this question sound non-rhetorical, as though she were genuinely curious.

Maria held the shovel still but did not withdraw it. "What do you want, Em." It wasn't a question. It was a line: fed to her and recited begrudgingly.

Em laughed—she laughed easily, and Maria felt she would've laughed at any response. "What do *I* want? Considerate. I'm sure you can guess. The same thing I've wanted for a decade, now." Em gestured at Mom's remains, and let the silence ring out for a while, filled only by a slight wind. "I'm getting it in a few weeks, you know. Eudaimon's sending my replacement."

"Congrats." Maria hadn't moved, was still tense, ready to do something, but not knowing anything that could be done.

"I'm going to be right over there." Em glanced lovingly in a seemingly arbitrary direction. "That's where my family's ascended. They saved me a spot." She turned back to face Maria. "I've got to deal with all this beforehand, though." At the word "this," she gestured widely at Maria's shovel, and pack, and self.

"No you don't," Maria said. "I've got it. You can head over early."

Another easy laugh. "You never liked me, did you? Though it's not about me, of course." Em looked downward. "It's about her." She continued looking downward, foregoing eye contact: as if this were not a real conversation between two people but a simple game, played to pass the time and not worth her full attention. "I'd been wondering when you would come out here. You've been building to it for months, with those walks you took. You know the drones see when you look at them, even discreetly. I only called them off today to save power; I already knew you were coming here."

Maria felt helpless, she was *helpless*. It weighed on her, doubled her exhaustion, and she wanted to collapse. She remained upright due only to the support of the shovel, now turned vertically, and by sheer force of rage. "Of course you did," she said. "Say more. I'm so predictable. You're so much better. You know better. Explain how you know everything, then lead me back to my cage." She gripped the shovel tighter. Maria knew she couldn't win a physical fight, but the shovel could make it close. She could do some damage if needed, particularly if she abandoned all concern for her own well-being.

Em shrugged. "I just thought you deserved to know." She walked, relaxed, past Maria, certainly noticing her tense stance but seeming to pay it no mind, and bent down to rifle through her pack, leaning against the other side of Mom's tombstone. She reached straight to the bottom, through the layer of distracting junk, and retrieved the bag of lime-green mold Maria had collected. She eyed it ponderously.

"Why are you *here?*" Maria said, and this time it was a question. Em was not acting remotely the way Maria had expected. She was being casual: playful, even. Maria had never been able to predict the way jellyheads acted, and the longer they'd gone before "ascending," the more bizarre their behavior could be. Being so close to ascension, Em—already eccentric—seemed to have let herself go to jelly more than ever before. This may be for the best: if Em had acted "normally," Maria would already be returning to the pain preserve, or perhaps dead. In her hopeless situation, any uncertainty was hope. "What's your goal in being here?" Maria asked, this time working to keep the anger out of her voice.

Em glanced at Maria, perhaps noticing the outward shift in mood, then continued eyeing the bag's lime-green contents. "I have to be," she said, gently squishing the bag. "It's my job. They won't ascend me otherwise, not since I became an ambassador. I have to do the job until my term's up or else they won't connect me. Or else I can't ascend without rotting away. And they *keep extending the term.*" She smiled softly, still staring at the mold. "I'm a hostage here. Same as you, really." Her eyes flicked to Maria: looking in her direction, but somehow not at her.

"I'm sorry," Maria said, and through sheer force of will, she mustered enough emotion to mean it. Though she still didn't fully understand, and she felt she needed to. "Couldn't you just stop wanting something, if you can't have it?"

Em vaguely smiled, or smiled vaguely. "I wish I could explain color to the blind," she said. "But I can only give hints." She seemingly thought for a moment, face unchanged. "Here: the hardest want to fulfill is the want to cease all wanting. Do you fulfill it or cause it to cease?" Another pause. "Does that answer your question?"

"I don't—"

"Oh, but you don't care, do you. You just want to clear this panel away." Suddenly animated, Em dropped the mold bag next to Maria's pack, then grabbed the side of Mom's tombstone that Maria had been crowbarring and pushed it across the blood-laden dirt until it almost touched the adjacent solar panel.

Maria stood dumbly, shovel still poised to pry away a stone that was no longer there. A few wires still ran from the center of where the tombstone had been, into the blood and the dirt.

Em walked over to the mold bag again and resumed pondering it as if nothing had happened.

Maria finally found words to express her shock. "What did you—why are you doing this?"

"You know," Em replied mid-ponder, "we aren't enemies. Eudaimon and the preserves. You're an essential part of our project.Allies. *I've* always thought, at least—though not everyone wants to keep you around."

Maria disliked the casual way in which Em referenced keeping her around. She felt like food being played with. "You *want* me to dig a hole here then?"

Em actually *shrugged.* "Is that what you want?"

Em didn't see Maria as a person, not really. Maria was some kind of lab experiment, and thus her questions didn't merit an answer.

But she wasn't stopping her. Maria thought it best not to waste a good thing.

She started digging.

The wires wouldn't lead into the jelly itself, just into a power source. Mom was installed with her head pointed east—they all were: all lined up—so Maria needed to dig about a meter eastward from the center of the wires. Her shovel met the mud. She step-jumped onto it, lifted it, and piled it to the side. Then she did it again.

"This mold is a puzzle, don't you think?" Em asked. Maria didn't look at her. "I always wondered why it never wanted to turn to joyjelly."

Dig. Step. Scoop. Dig. Step. Scoop.

"There were other versions, you know, that actually *ate away* at the jelly. Eudaimon didn't develop those further of course—but I wonder, sometimes, if they should have. The jelly was actively *choosing* to become that mold: what must it be like to be that kind of mold? Would it be even better than ascension?" Her voice was giddy at the thought. Maybe her face, too; Maria did not look.

Dig. Step. Scoop. Dig. Step. Scoop.

"Because that's the issue, isn't it?" Em continued, unbothered by Maria's preoccupation. "We'll always need people who aren't jelly. Me. You. Because what if we got it wrong? What if joyjelly is just a local optimum? What if there's an even *better* thing to be? Then we're dooming the world to an imperfect fate."

Dig. Step. Scoop. Dig. Step. Scoop.

"But as long as you're around, there's still a chance you'll find it. The true best way to be." Em paused. "Or your descendants could."

Farther down, the dirt became muddier. Bloodier. Bloody enough now that Maria was uncomfortable. She didn't want to slice right into the brain—not quite yet. She dropped the shovel, kneeled, and began clearing the rest of the mud away with her hands. Slowly, carefully. She could feel Em staring at her intently, and Maria stared intently elsewhere.

"You're being cautious," Em noted. "Uncertain. Good. That's part of your job in all this. To not know."

Maria's fingertips pressed into something distinctly fleshy and undiggable. She withdrew immediately. Then, gingerly, she cleared the rest of the dirt away, until she saw it, sitting there. Mom's brain. It was warm to the touch and pulsed faintly.

This was too much—it was right there, *she* was *right there.*

Em made a sound as if to say something, and Maria snapped her head to glare at her intently. This was a reverent moment, and Em shouldn't be here for it. Em broke eye contact. Regarded the mold again, unspeaking.

Maria felt hot tears welling up in her eyes unbidden, tried pushing them down, but she couldn't control them, she could never control them: she was her mother's daughter, after all. She stopped trying to control them, and let them fall onto the jelly:

And so, part of her joined her mother, just like she'd asked.

For several minutes, she wept quietly. Staring at Mom. Then she moved, delicately: clearing the mud, making a radius the size of an aspen sapling, plus a little more. More brain was revealed now than Mom had ever had initially, but some of what was here was really Mom. Maria placed her palm on it, and felt the pulse, breathed with it. With her.

Maria stood slowly and fetched the shovel.

Em, who had been gazing serenely at an apple core from Maria's dinner for the past few minutes, spoke up now. "Do you think she'll be happier this way?"

Maria walked up to the hole she had dug.

"Or do you just not think that way."

Maria glared at Em, then turned downward again.

"You know if you dig into the jelly itself, you'll just be killing her."

Maria gripped the shovel tighter. She steadied her breath.

"She wouldn't want that."

"You didn't know her." Quietly.

"She chose ascension. She left behind no documents suggesting—"

"You *didn't know* her." No longer quiet.

"I'm worried you're allowing your naïve emotions to cloud your judgment."

"You don't know me, either." Maria was letting Em distract her, she knew, and perhaps that was Em's goal. But the distraction felt good. It kept her from thinking about what she was about to do. Postpone it, for a little longer.

Em smiled sadly, patiently, as if at an obstinate toddler who hadn't been listening. "Maria," she said. "I know you very well. I know how much you hate Eudaimon, and hate me. I know how close you were with your mother. I know you've been planning this for months. I know you purposely delayed taking this morning's medication until early this afternoon when your hike was already underway. Presumably because you wanted to stay even-headed late into the night." At this, Em pulled a bottle of pills from Maria's pack. She brandished them gently.

Maria was silent—unsure of what she ought to say. This was a test, and she felt that perhaps if she said the right answers, Em might let her be. But Maria didn't know what the answers were, so she merely listened.

Em tried to nudge her further. "You're already managing your brain states, is what I mean," she said. "You already know how beneficial it is. You understand."

Maria's eyes drifted uneasily to the pill bottle: Em shouldn't be that close to them, some panicked part of her thought, she could mess with them, slip a replica into the bottle that's full of nanobots, change Maria into—

"Maria," Em said. "Eudaimon owns the manufacturers that supply your pills." She'd noticed Maria's glance and predicted her thoughts. "They own everything. You think they couldn't just give you whatever they want? If they wanted to alter your pills—and they don't—they wouldn't need me here to do so." She sighed. "Despite what you think, I'm not interested in undermining your freedom. I actually want to enhance it." She tossed the bottle back into Maria's pack.

"What do you mean." Gather more information: find out what to say to appease her. To make her leave.

Em reached out toward Maria, then balled her fists, as if she wanted to take her hands but knew better. "I . . . Maria, I want you to be the best version of yourself, that's all. And I don't think that's who you are right now. I think you know that, too."

"What do you mean."

Em sighed that particular jellyhead sigh—the one that was only performatively sad, where the sadness didn't reach the eyes. "I know you've tried to quit your pills. Four times now, since you've lived on the preserve.

"But you can't—you get too dysfunctional, or too anxious. So you start back up again. But then you try to quit." Em paused. "I just don't understand—*why*? Why do you want to quit, if they help you feel better? To *be* better? I know the side effects are minimal. *You* know the side effects are minimal. They just—all they do is help you do what you want with your life. I half-understand not wanting the treatment I have—but why not even this?"

" . . . You want me to do what I want with my life?"

"Yes, Maria. I really do."

"If I asked you to leave right now, would you?"

Em seemed to think about it—though perhaps this was performative as well. "Yes."

"And would you tell your successor about this conversation? About what happened here? The person sent to replace you?"

"I'm required to."

"Would you?"

" . . . No." Em laughed wildly at her own answer.

Maria smiled at this, too. "Okay. Em?"

"Yes, Maria?" She was beaming.

"I'd like you to leave now. It's important for—for my freedom. For becoming the best me."

"Okay," Em said and nodded collegially. She stretched, seemingly in preparation to walk back to the preserve. "I hope you believe what you're saying. Because I do." Her eyes flashed briefly with something fear-like. "But don't—you don't talk about it either. Don't tell people. At least not until—I can't have my term extended again. I can't."

Maria nodded. "I understand," she said, and she did. Fear of Eudaimon was a sentiment of Em's, finally, that she could truly relate to. "I'm not telling anybody."

Em nodded back. "I can't," she repeated. The fear-like flash vanished from her eyes, and she smiled once more at Maria before turning away. She began walking, then paused, briefly, turning her head halfway back. "Apple trees work better, anyway," she said, then faced away from Maria and walked, turning back no more. She disappeared quickly into the darkness.

Maria was left alone with this cryptic comment, her bag, her shovel, and silence.

And Mom.

Maria placed her palm on her again, and again felt her heartbeat. Did it quicken at her touch?

She knelt down beside her and leaned over—mud and blood fully soaked her clothes. She leaned into the hole, placed her ear where her palm had been, and she heard her heartbeat, too.

It was the beat of all of them of course, sharing the same blood, the same current, driven by turbines deep underground.

But it was Mom's heartbeat.

She was going to cut into it. That would make it stop, at least right here. At least in the part that was Mom.

She stood and fetched the shovel. Hovered it above Mom.

A thought pushed itself into her awareness, against her best efforts: *will it hurt?* She faltered and wondered if she had the strength to do this.

There's pain. But pain doesn't hurt. Not if I don't want.

Maria breathed deeply in, then deeply out. It was time.

She touched the shovel tip gently to Mom's surface.

. . . no, she should fetch the tree first.

She retracted the shovel.

Dropped it.

She walked over to her backpack and reached in to retrieve the tree, cursing her own cowardice. *That's your job in all this—to not know.* Em's words echoed. She felt manipulated, briefly, then it faded because these words rang true.

Eudaimon wouldn't have faltered. If they decided that aspens were better than joyjelly, they would bulldoze every brain in their care, planting aspens in their wake, and feel no remorse. They wouldn't have taken the care to trek out and plant them, one by one, burying them amongst sleeping bags and mattress pads and other signs of over-preparation, in a bag stuffed so full that the sapling itself was difficult to find, where was it, and then if they made a new joyjelly that was better than aspens, they'd bulldoze the aspens and plant the jelly all over again, and it'd be just the same to them because they didn't really care about people, didn't care about Mom, were so damn sure of themselves that they were sending things out into space soon, starting the process on the Moon first, and the ocean floor, and then eventually everywhere, because "everywhere on Earth" wasn't enough, it had to be Everywhere, and the mold was here, and the soil was there, and her fingers scraped the bottom of her pack, and she dumped it all out, all into the mud, and the

Tree

Wasn't

There.

It wasn't there.

She hadn't packed it.

She had forgotten.

It was back in her room. Next to the coffee grounds she'd saved for compost and left sitting there too.

Just sitting there.

Maria fell to her knees and was still.

Just sitting there.

The wind blew.

It picked up some of her lighter possessions, scattered as they were, and began to carry them off.

The Eudaimon pamphlet fluttered away.

Maria sat in the mud.

Stupidly.

Being herself: stupid.

She sat and sat and sat.

Eventually, her mind restarted, and she became aware of the situation: herself, sitting stupidly, in the mud and the blood and her mother's brain. Then she became aware of her awareness, of her reaction to this stupid sitting: she became aware of a deep despair. Too deep to fathom, too deep to even fully feel.

Her eyes, free to wander as they pleased because nothing really mattered, settled on her pill bottle, flung to the side on a relatively dry section of mud.

A version of Em that existed solely in Maria's head spoke to her: *If you had taken it this morning, you'd have remembered. You'd have the tree with you.*

"Fuck you, Em," she said. Matter-of-factly.

Mom would have found this entire situation hilarious. She'd never have let Maria hear the end of it.

"Fuck you, Mom," she said. Quietly, lovingly.

Her despair deepened then. Reached the bottom. Crashed through, wrapped around, and came in from the other side.

Maria laughed.

She laughed and laughed and laughed.

It sounded like Mom's laugh, of course, like Mom was joining in, with her old laugh, the true one: but weren't they really the same?

Her eyes wandered again, free to do as they pleased because there was nothing that didn't matter, they couldn't pick wrong, and this time they settled on the discarded apple core.

Imaginary-Em spoke again, this time quoting her real-life counterpart: *apple trees work better, anyway.*

"Fuck *you*, Em," Maria repeated, this time with a slight tone of affection. She cackled madly at the audacity. She sounded insane, and so cackled again. She scrambled over to the core, grabbed it, held it close, hugged it. Cracked it open, gingerly pulled out the seeds. Selected the best one: it was difficult, they were all so beautiful, so full of potential, but this one, this one here was perfect.

She clutched it tightly with one hand, and with the other, she spread the mold onto Mom's brain: prepare it, help it accept the eventual tree. She piled the mud she had dug back on top: it needed to be planted shallower, needed to germinate before its roots reached down. The roots would reach the brain eventually, but it would take time. And when they reached it . . .

It might not work. Even with the mold, they might not grow further. The joyjelly might halt their progress.

But it might let them in.

It would have to choose. Mom would have to choose: *do you want to stay like this—or do you want to become something new?*

Maria placed the seed and piled the mud gently on top. It would grow if it wanted, and then the rest would be up to Mom.

Maria picked up her shovel and smoothed over the area where the seed had been planted. Picked up her pack. Picked up the apple core, removed the rest of the seeds, and threw each in a different direction: cross-pollinators. Let other parts of the jelly choose, too. Picked up the rest of the wind-scattered trash still within reach: old habits. Picked up her pills and sighed to herself: at herself. Tried wiping the mud off the pills onto her already fully mud-laden shirt, to little success. Chuckled. Placed them gingerly back into the bag and resolved to be less stubborn about them in the future: at least for a while. Though she and Eudaimon had very different thoughts about what her "best self" looked like—perhaps these were a part of that self.

Maria packed up everything else. She made it look, as much as possible, like she'd never been there. For all Eudaimon knew, these seeds had fallen naturally, or perhaps were never there.

"Bye, Mom," Maria said, and walked home.

The wind blew behind her.

ABOUT THE AUTHOR

Grant Collier is able to peel an entire mandarin orange in one piece, without any breaks, at least seventy-five percent of the time. When left to his own devices, he can be found reading, writing stories such as this one, playing music, or climbing on a plastic rock. He has previously obtained degrees in Physics and Philosophy, and is currently pursuing a PhD in Machine Learning, but swears it will be his last degree. He lives in Durham, NC with his wife and their dog. This is his first publication.

Stellar Evolutions in Pop Idol Artistry
EM X. LIU

Out there, the crowd is waiting. Mingming knows they must be—vaster and hungrier than any he has seen so far in his career—but all he can make out is a dark mass, rolling, rushing, rising to reach him where they think he will appear. His breathing comes harsh and labored in his own ears. For a moment, the air on Ceres is thick with smog and anticipation—fuck the atmosphere gas titration! When Mingming inhales, the crowd moves with him as one being, made up only of want.

Sound billows around him, a solid thing. Music and cheering layered together, bass and wails. It drills into him, busts something frantic open in his sternum. The crowd shouts, cries out, loves him, wants him. Mingming breathes. Heat sloughs off the thin layer of coolant sealed over his skin, pouring out of him in waves and adding only to the frenzy. He bites his tongue and makes up his mind. His reinforced bones let him take advantage of Ceres' ninety-seven percent pared gravity to leap over the carefully calibrated springboard entirely and launch himself, up and up and out.

A falling sweep of light blinds him first. Mingming crests, caught in the beam.

And then—

Cut all that bullshit. As in, the dopamine rush addict high of nearly a hundred thousand people, calling your name. That's not important. Mingming forgets the drip eventually.

What he never forgets is this: the split second when the lights flicker off, and he sees. Faces turned up, too small to make out, but everyone reverent. It's the only time he's ever felt the numbers in a way that was real. All those people, witnessing something they've made beautiful. He's never sure if he means himself or his music, but it doesn't matter.

Mingming knows exactly what he wants here.

He wants them to listen.

He wants to be glorious.

"Mingming," Jora had said in a half-whisper, three cycles ago.

Mingming's mind was groggy. His limbs were not his own, but it was always like that immediately after thaw. He dragged himself upward, scrubbing at the back of his freshly shorn undercut. "What's wrong?"

Around the dorm, everyone else's cryopods were humming along peacefully. He was the only one awake.

Manager Jora looked chagrined. "No," he said. "We need to have a conversation."

"Just us?"

"It's about your contract."

Mingming's brow furrowed. "Is it urgent?" Barely a few stops into their tenth galactic tour, there was still so much to do.

"Yes," said Jora. "Please, let's go somewhere more private."

On the eighth day of Prime month 03, year 2011 P.E., Yang Junming—handsome, bright, Mingming for the fans—debuts into the golden era of idolhood. Any later and the next generation of idolbots will have finally been perfected with the right amount of spontaneity to encourage an optimal level of parasocial bonding. Any earlier, and he'd have been another bright kid with a dream bigger than his home galaxy, too fragile to survive the freeze-thaw cryo cycles necessary for intergalactic touring.

Mingming had worked for that moment for nearly a decade of grueling training, his spark of vocal talent plucked from a humble Ceresian origin out of millions of hopefuls from galaxy-Prime alone, nurtured into something worthy of stardom. He trains longer than most and his fans call him hardworking. He is as exceptional as he was made to be.

Fast-forward approximately three years, four months, and twenty-two days, give or take a few solar days depending on how you calculate. Lunar Flare had made it big enough that they have a private star-ship this time. Mingming is, predictably, holed up in the practice room. By his calculations, there are three and a half cameras aimed at him. The most obvious is mounted on top of the dance room mirror. Another flits around, a beetle-sized drone glutting itself on all sorts of unflattering—but candid!—angles. The third swivels from outside the ceiling-high wall, grabbing a wide-angle shot like an old painting: Mingming's solitary reaching form inside the practice room, trapped behind a prism glass wall and lonely against the signature undulations of Beta-Tau-54Y's Typhoon nebula.

The next one he counts as a half because it's not recording. The monitor is embedded in his cornea, without the telltale mild lemon-electric-hum that would mean Jora is watching him drill the tricky bits of the title track choreo that he still shamefully messes up every few runs. He's learned by now to ignore the surveillance, but sometimes he forgets, and the slimy reminder makes everything else in the room surreal, plasticked over. His brain glitches. He can't even remember how to move his own fingers.

The door opens with a hiss, and Mingming nearly falls over.

"Bad news!" Antares declares, sneakers squeaking over the fresh laminated floor as he barges in without more of a greeting. "Holy shit, are you still practicing? Jora is going to *kill* us."

Hwang Antares is probably the closest friend he has in the group. But Mingming would never say that unless under threat of death. They were nothing alike: Antares is pretty and a self-professed narcissist, born for idolhood in a way that Mingming has always had to work for; Mingming is a workaholic with a perfectionist streak that made him an outright asshole during training. He's self-aware enough to know that. They've stuck with each other so long because Mingming never has to explain himself and Antares knows when not to ask.

Today, he looks frazzled, which is fairly uncharacteristic.

Mingming straightens. "Hm."

"I'm serious," Antares says. "We're in so much fucking trouble."

"What's going on?" Mingming spares half a glance at the speaker still blaring "Cosmotastic Glow" loud enough that his mild tone can barely be heard properly.

Antares paces. "There was supposed to be a show tonight!" he explains. "Taixing-nan lost their bid for the tour list, but *apparently* the company negotiated a mocap concert instead, and *apparently* Jora told us day one, but he forgot to key it into the schedule, and I know you never check Orbital, but the Taixing fan club is pissed, and if we don't hop on feed to literally grovel right the fuck now, we're screwed—"

"Okay," Mingming says.

"Are you even—"

Mingming grabs Antares' wrist to calm his frantic gesturing, then counts two easy beats in his head before reaching out to press his palm against Antares' chest. The fourth and now last camera in the room is caught in his grasp, a jewel-shaped device that camouflages neatly with the other gaudy buttons on Antares' shirt.

"Goddammit." Immediately, Antares' demeanor changes. Loosened jaw, loosened shoulders. He finger-combs his hair back into order, then pointedly rolls his eyes. "I should've realized when *you* of all people were being too fucking calm. How do you *always* know?"

"You're a terrible actor. Do we even have mocaps in our contracts?"

"If Jora has his way, it'll get written in when we renew. It was *his* idea. He wanted more footage for the docuseries and thought this would be a good bit or something."

"You should've tried it on Sol."

"That would be mean, come on. Hidden cameras are only fun if there's an actual chance we could be caught."

Mingming uncovers the camera so he can flash it his most charming grin. "Tell Antares to try harder next time, sir," he says. "I can give him some lessons if you mark it into our schedule."

Antares bats him away. He rips the camera out of his shirt like Jora wouldn't freak at the damaged goods, and Mingming, finally, is caught off guard. Antares grins, all lazy and smug, the fake one that annoys Mingming the most because of how cheesy it is. "Stop fucking around and take a break with me."

"That doesn't make any sense."

"You're not going to learn anything in the next hour that you haven't already, and we're due for reconditioning at oh-three-hundred sharp, buddy. Have you even gotten any sleep since we docked?"

No. "Sure."

Antares doesn't believe him—this has been a ritual between them since the very first time that Antares found him nearly passed out on the floor of their training days practice rooms, pale and feverish from exerting himself too soon post-op. His bones had been shinier, sturdier, but the rest of him hadn't caught up, yet. Antares called him an idiot and spent the next day sneaking him antibiotics so he'd stitch himself back together in time for evals. They both had gotten in trouble because evals went, predictably, terribly, but for the first time, Mingming didn't hate himself so much for it. So, when Antares calls, Mingming goes.

Before they badge out of the limited employees-only section of the tour ship, Antares signals for him to duck into a small alcove. Mingming holds his tongue when Antares ducks to don a mask, then allows him to press one over Mingming's cheeks, too. He closes his eyes as the light silica settles over his nose, cheeks, chin—shifts his fine-boned features and renders them unrecognizable. The subterfuge should be something he's used to by now, but an involuntary shiver of paranoid anticipation rolls through him, nevertheless.

"We'd get in trouble," Mingming murmurs.

"Who's gonna know."

"Maybe that stalker who hacked into your feed last year has a catalog of every mask you own, you don't know."

Antares scowls. "The company banned them."

Mingming doesn't offer the obvious counterpoint, which is that stalker-fans are notoriously adept at dodging even personal biometric-based bans, which means that there are probably a nonsignificant percentage of them wandering the public space out beyond the practice section. SZGY³ was a company of fine resource management—they knew how to keep fans happy. Only the most passionate paid to be part of the crew ship, after all, joining them on their schedule from stop to stop, the ultimate way to follow your idol on tour. From cryo to planet-hopping with less than twenty-four hours to spend in each place, they'd understand the whole exhausting experience.

They weren't technically supposed to hide from the fans, but there were plenty of things Jora didn't have to know about. Not that it would be a problem, hopefully, in the middle of the night.

Antares pulls his choppy bob out of its messy tie and shoves Mingming through the door. Instantly, the sights and sounds overwhelm him. It smells like a real street, out here. There's greenery. The bird sounds are piped in from above, but it's real enough. Mingming rubs his suddenly goosefleshed arms, realizing with a wince that the relative isolation of their dorms and the practice room had masked how bad his post-thaw actually is. The climate mod is chilly, and the draft blows right through him. He aches in places he doesn't even remember could still ache. He must look haggard. The aesthetician is going to have a field day with him tomorrow.

There's no need for Antares to say *I told you so.* He shoves his hand into Mingming's hoodie pocket, steering them forward. "Remember when we used to sneak out as trainees?"

Mingming snorts. "You mean when you'd *kidnap* me."

"Mmmhm," answers Antares without a beat, "exactly. Don't you miss it?"

Training had been an endless grind of dance and vocal lessons, interspersed by media training and crash courses of the cultural practices of each system that SZGY³ was contracted with. Mingming doesn't remember any details because every day was the same. His body was different, then. Still fragile, ready to collapse after only twelve hours of practice. But the sweating made simple sense: they were working toward something bigger than each other.

"Yeah," Mingming says. "Every day."

They push into a small corner store, set into the wall in a section of the ship that doesn't get any windows. This is truer to their shared memory: they came to age stuck on a floating rock that could barely be called an asteroid—there was no star in that system, so heat and light both were artificial flickering things. In retrospect, SZGY³ had owned everything, so the corner store latched onto the side of their training gym was mostly to appease the hundreds of kids stuck inside, a controlled rebellion that the company allowed. It kept them human, if not sane.

"You seem off," Antares says.

They buy shitty freeze-dried ramen. Mingming wants to tear into his, but he knows it'll only make him sick. He shrugs. "Remembering," he says.

Antares leans back on the counter. "I miss it, too." He looks worse than Mingming had assumed. His wrists are thinner than Mingming remembers. Antares is all bluster and showmanning, but it's not like he doesn't have his demons. Mingming pretends he doesn't notice his fingers trembling when he picks at his gritty noodle pieces. Touring is hard on them all.

"Do you know what's happening after this album?" he asks, all of a sudden.

Mingming blinks. "No."

"Our contract is coming up." The way Antares says it, it's like he knows about that conversation Jora pulled him into, three shows and cycles ago, that he's done his level best to forget since.

So, Mingming ignores him.

As always, Antares barrels forward. "Do you regret anything?"

"No," Mingming answers automatically.

Antares tosses his head back to empty the bag into his mouth. His teeth crunch against the ramen. "But, like, do you ever think about what else you'd be doing?"

"No," Mingming says again, even quicker.

Antares rolls his eyes. "Figures you'd say that."

"What else is worth doing?"

"*And* that."

"I'm serious," Mingming says. He tosses his snack out, ignoring his stomach's cramping. "It's like, you know, nothing easy is worth—"

"I'm pretty sure the saying is nothing worth doing is easy," Antares cuts in, his mouth a stubborn line.

Mingming disagrees. They're quiet. There's nothing more to say. The year before debut, when Sol had been added to the lineup, Jora had to step in when Mingming had grilled him to near tears during a rough recording session. It was the first and only time he and Antares had fought. *Don't be like that,* Antares had said, fierce, *he's just a kid.* Mingming's heart thumped in his chest. His mouth soured. *What's the point,* he'd said, *if he won't take it seriously? Did he think it'd be easy?* There was nothing to say after that, either. Sol had figured it out. He grew up. Mingming, privately, felt vindicated, and Antares had never brought it up again.

Outside, the artificial light is starting to creep in. Impulsively, Mingming takes the mask off, and as they trek back to the dorm to prep for reconditioning, the streets slowly fill up, murmurs and whispers trailing them until, by the time they reach their destination, it's impossible to hear the clamor of his own thoughts over the shouts for him anymore.

Concert day arrives with an exhale of relief. His body is scrubbed raw by the processing. His skin remains dewy. They step out into the atmosphere-controlled dome of the Aurum System's Centurian Stadium as one, all of Lunar Flare hand in hand: Sol and Antares and Mingming and Xenon and Neul, a unit greater than the sum of its parts, their cohesion years in the making.

He forgets the exhaustion and not the choreography, blends in with his members like a bird in a murmuration. Look at that—all the drilling, worth every second. Then—one hour in, and it's time for his solo stage. He's already dizzy, a scratch in his throat. All his hard work has brought him to where he is standing, alone in the middle of the stage save for the live band. He'd thrown out hundreds of songs until he realized that his first solo needed to be about the truest thing he knows.

Mingming's only ever felt certain in two places. Before debut, he knew the practice room, where effort translated well to result, and his bruised-up knees were a metric of how much he wanted it. He collected those bruises as proudly as he collected his concrit, spending an hour longer for every stray comment any of the trainers made. Eventually, the pain resolved into a cold but certain clarity. After their first showcase, he understood—that cold flame was meant to nurture *this.*

This, bright and searing, the stage stretching out into where it's dark.

This, chest heaving, sweat dripping, everything.

This, the white-hot knife of clarity that cleaves through any doubt he's ever had.

"I'd like to share a new song with you all tonight," he murmurs into his mic, a sweet confession for thousands. His voice echoes, expands. The crowd screams in approval. Behind him, the drums kick off, nice and crisp. Mingming jumps in a beat early, and they're fucking off, rolling into the song hard and fast. The music is in and around him, in his shoulders and his fingertips. Mingming's the one who drives it forward. The song has a heartbeat and it's his, pounding steady—he sings about that cold flame, the blue burn—*bum, ba-da-dum, dum.*

He swears the front row is singing along when he eases back, lets the song breathe. The album was a week ago, but it always feels like everyone is singing along. He leans into his mic, sings low alongside his own backing track, his whole body convinced of it. He shakes his hair loose from his face and someone out there wolf whistles. Mingming's laughing by the time the last note strikes.

His body wants to cry. His tear ducts are intact, allowing him the full range of emotion, but he never uses them unless he's on tour—pure physiological reaction. He's overwhelmed, drained out. He cries and the rest of the group runs out, Neul patting his back and Antares coaxing the crowd into heckling him, and then he's laughing again, more, through the tears. "Thank you!" he shouts to the sound of cheers and cheers and cheers, and he believes them. Sometimes it's that simple.

When he stumbles offstage, he turns and throws up. "Whoa, whoa," says Antares, catching him. Mingming spits, bile dripping from his lip. He leans over his own knees, vision swimming.

"It's fine," he insists. "I'm fine."

Again. Arms open, eyes dry, throat wrecked.

Again. Mingming's ears pop; he's stuffed up with adrenaline. Every tour is hard like this, he tells himself. In the back of his mind, he thinks about Jora's meeting. He wonders: is it worth it?

Again.

Again.

"I'm sorry to do this so abruptly, but I think you deserve to know," is what Jora started with. Mingming stared at him, dull, barely comprehending. "Sorry," Jora said. He placed his hands flat on the table, and Mingming knew then that his contrite expression was a true thing. "I'm not supposed to be doing this. But . . . We've worked together well, haven't we? I'd like to think I know you, a bit. I hope that's not presumptuous."

"What's going on?" The dread trickled in slowly. It was true that Jora knew him better than most, but he wasn't sure what that had to do with anything.

"They're planning for auditions," Jora said, "which means it'll be soon that they're going to reassign you. Knowing you . . . I wanted to make sure you knew what was going on. That's all. Your contract is up."

His mouth was dry. If it had to do with the contract, he couldn't wrap his head around why no one else was here. "I thought I already said I want to renew."

"It'll have to be renegotiated."

"What?"

"The Eclipse branch wants you back."

"I'm sorry?" The Eclipse branch managed actors, not idols. And as far as Mingming remembered, his contract had nothing to do with them. That area of the entertainment world was as distant to him as normalcy was, to be truthful. Neul sometimes said that he'd just become an actor if this whole idolhood thing didn't work out, which always irritated Mingming for no real reason.

Jora sighed. "There's no real way to say this, is there?"

"Stop being cryptic to avoid hurting my feelings," Mingming snapped.

"Your name isn't Yang Junming," Jora told him.

Kang Linjun had once been the face of a phenomenon—it just wasn't a very nice one. He'd been picked up from Ceres for his pretty face, and it was rare enough to find any talent at all from the belt population, so people paid some attention to the feed dramas that he started in. Gutter shows, basically. Boys' love dramas that raked in credits, that made Linjun feel sticky inside with shame. But still, it was a career. And he was, by some small metric, a star, the way he'd always wanted. Idol-actor, they called him, which stung, because Linjun had never shared his background of failed auditions and the secret drive of songs, the childhood dream that died a quiet death when his sister grew ill, and he realized he had to stop wasting his time and energy on trying for a crapshoot. Just his luck to be scouted for something else entirely at his second barista gig. He knew the casting directors always picked him for how pleasant he was to look at instead of how convincing he was in moving them to feel. Feed-dwellers and the general populace all agreed the sort of trash he acted in wasn't worth paying attention to in any serious manner.

Untethered Amongst Stars blows up in unexpected measure, so popular that it careens Linjun and his costar both into mainstream popularity. He renegotiates a real, working contract with SZGY³ Eclipse that seems to treat him as a person and not a disposable thing. His agent gets a dozen scripts overnight, from writers who had openly disdained Linjun's work—not directly, but they'd all participated in the brewing discourse. He reads them and cries. He feels part of something bigger than himself for the first time.

He's cast in Amna Song Narabit's next feature. Linjun doesn't believe the news at first. Her directorial debut *The Populist* was the Halla Festival finalist of that year; when he squeezed in an afternoon to see it in a vintage-style theater, he thought—*maybe*—maybe this could be worth it. The headlines are sensational: VIRAL FEED ACTOR THE RIGHT FIT FOR NEXT SONG FILM? They use words that say one thing—populist, adolescent—and mean another—who the fuck cast this sellout pretty boy who only starred in unrealistic gay drivel for what could be the film of a century?

So, of course, two days after the casting announcement, the news breaks. KANG LINJUN CAUGHT IN SORDID LOVE AFFAIR? The biggest sin is not that he was sleeping with a man, but that it wasn't his *Untethered Amongst Stars* costar, who half the galaxy was convinced he was in love with. A day after that, rumors about drug use start circulating, and no matter how much untruth there is in it, Linjun knows it's fucking over.

"Don't worry," says his agent, frazzled but sure-faced. "We'll take care of you."

On the twenty-ninth day of Prime month 01, year 2009 P.E., Yang Junming wakes up in the SZGY³ Occultation Branch idol dorms, and he is a different person. His face rings a bell to some, but with some light work, he looks enough like a handful of other fresh new boys to diffuse the resemblance to his former self. He remembers five years of training that he has not lived through. His dormmates, Hwang Antares amongst them, have the same set of memories. Two years out from debut and the team is nearly settled already, which leaves only three other minds to tamper with—by the time Sol arrives, he's solidified in the pack. No one in their dorm knows much about Kang Linjun, other than that it was kind of a shitty story. That's what fame does to you, Neul says solemnly, and carefully, nobody talks about the fate they're all working toward.

When Antares wakes, he tells Junming—who is not Mingming yet—that he should skip practice with him, but manager Jora comes in to inform them that Junming is about to enroll in advanced dance classes, which means he has no more time in his schedule to play truant. Junming had joined the team off the strength of his vocals and his hidden talent as a producer. It hadn't seemed strange, that he didn't know how to dance, really, despite the fact that plenty of trainees had been axed for that very reason. There's an irony—Mingming would've been the first to cry unfair if he'd known he effectively skipped every ruthless audition and eval.

He learns to dance. He's not good, but he's passable. He writes. There's something stuck in his heart that he needs to learn how to extricate. He comes close, but he never figures it out. Antares teases him for his serious face, and he doesn't know how to respond. Antares aces every evaluation when Mingming has to practice so long, he sneaks out to vomit at the end of every day. He tries not to hate Antares for it. He pushes away, but Antares always bounces back.

And now, three years later, they've yet to be sick of each other.

"We haven't been back to Prime in a while," says Antares. They're about to go to sleep, already tucked in nice and cozy in their synthsuits and strapped to the cryobed. Mingming's body is scrubbed soft again, ready for the next show.

He doesn't remember how long it's been, either, but that doesn't really mean anything. "Antares," he says, and Antares startles because he's never this direct. Still, no matter how long Mingming holds his glinty-eyed gaze, Antares never flinches. "Do you remember the night before we debuted?"

Antares laughs. "When we got shit-faced and tried to take the company ship on a joyride?"

"Do you remember what I asked you?"

The hum of their ship's machinery has never been louder. Antares shifts. "Why are you talking about this now?"

"Antares," says Mingming again, "Please." And maybe it's his voice, so quiet he's hoarse, but Antares finally flinches.

"You asked me if this was forever for me." Antares looks pained. "And then I said yes, because of course I fucking said yes, and then you asked me why."

"Tell me again," says Mingming.

This must be a true memory, though it feels no less than all the others. Mingming has spent the last five cycles sorting through, and he has yet to be able to find the tells, any real cracks. The two of them, alone, picking at the lock of their manager's ship. Eventually, they'd given up and sat shoulder to shoulder outside the hangar. They'd wanted to see the sun—that is, *the* sun, the star of galaxy-Prime, the first one—but they had to settle for the day-loop light cresting over the artificial horizon of their training grounds. They'd drank to that, anyway. Delirious and young and drunk with eternity. That was real. It had to be.

Antares worries at his cheek. His shoulders are half an inch lower than they usually are, when he's puffed up and proud for Jora, for their fans. "I want to be loved," he finally says. "It's the same now as it's always been. But that's not serious enough for you, is it?"

Mingming's never told him this, but the reason he always knows when they try to nail him with a hidden camera is not because he has some eagle-eyed instinct for how to spot a lens, but that Antares shrinks in on himself when he knows he's being filmed. It's different than the version of him on stage, big and bold and vibrant.

Mingming wants to climb out of his pod. Antares' eyes must be shuttered. Self-conscious doesn't belong on his features, and Mingming needs him to know this. How could you not love him? But the timer to launch is starting, and they have to go, so he settles for the firmest voice he can muster. "No," he says, "I think it's the most serious thing in the world."

"No," Mingming said. He stood up. He clenched his fists. "Absolutely not. No."

"Mingming," Jora said. "We've already started the audition process for your replacement. It won't be quite the same—you've really made quite an idol out of yourself in the meantime, that was a surprise. We're all very proud of you at the company. But, well—the script's been stuck in development since Narabit is still interested, and that's a much better opportunity, still. You have quite a lot more potential, they think, as an actor."

"What?" Mingming blurted. "I don't care about that."

"That's because you don't remember it," Jora said gently. "I'm going to be blunt: the only reason they're offering this to you is because Narabit insisted. Otherwise, we'd be holding auditions for the next Kang Linjun and not the next Yang Mingming. She said she wanted *you*—I don't even know how she knew about, you know, all this."

"Why all this in the first place?" Mingming asked, desperate. "Why didn't you just bench me."

Jora patted him on the back. "Honestly, Linjun—you were smart. From what I know—and it's not my department, so don't quote me, I guess—but they would've if your big shot lawyers hadn't threatened the company with breach of contract."

Maybe Kang Linjun loved what he did. Or maybe he knew he had to be vigilant. He knew—Mingming knew—that everybody was disposable, actors and idols both.

"Why . . . why *this*, then?" Mingming gestured at himself, the way his body was already starting to hurt. The rest of his members, sleeping still. The quiet hum of the ship, sailing silently through the cosmos. This life, all of it. All the effort that went into making it real: the work of categorizing his own memories, of rebuilding him ground up, the re-debut, so as to give him something while his former self rehabilitated.

Jora shrugged. "Think you asked for it. Dahye—your agent—really wanted to do you a favor. Anyway, really think about it. More than enough time has passed, you've been on hiatus so long that the public has long since lost interest. I've heard the Narabit script is beautiful. You're not going back to feed-dramas, you're going back to the start of a real career."

Even after Antares begs off, Mingming waits until the last possible second to put himself into cryo. He wants to remember every moment of this. The tour picks up speed, after this next stop. Tomorrow, they enter galaxy-Prime's territory. The ship will drop off their groupie fans, and after that, they'll head for the far reaches of the galactics—this is the biggest tour that SZGY³ has ever organized for Lunar Flare.

Did Linjun always want something different? Mingming can visualize those days, if he tries. It would be like shooting an MV, but longer, more involved. Truthfully, he hates shooting schedules. He never knows if it's a good day or bad. The director walks them around, he does his best. That slimy feeling is everywhere, the camera's lens slithering over his body, immortalizing this moment. The reaction comes months later. It's nothing like the stage. The cold loneliness of practice only ever feels worth it in the heat of an audience. Releasing new music always leaves him feeling greasy inside, slick with anxiety, until he knows how it's being heard. It's never real until the first performance, a starburst of sound to make it true.

He closes his eyes. His palms are calloused. There are imperfections even the relentless treatments and prepping can't erase. There's a seed of a memory, small and imperfect, buried deep in his brain.

He's eight years old and Ceres is at war. In the grand scheme of things, no one remembers the striking days of the Ceresian miners, but if you lived it, the world might as well have been ending. People dropping of lungrot—his father, his brother, his own name on the line. The demonstrations went on long past his bedtime, but one night, his life changes. This memory is crystal clear. His throat is sore from the unfortunate cold he picked up from Baba yesterday. The roar around him is louder than his own thoughts. Everyone's chanting, their voices blending together into a cacophony of revolt. Out of the din comes the solitary slick wail of electric guitar. Baba hoists him up so they can watch I-CHOR's J Gong—leader, frontman, not Ceresian-born, but the best guitarist who's ever come out of the Belt, so they all claimed him anyway. He rises out of the undulating crowd.

I-CHOR is the greatest band that SZGY[3] will ever produce. (Later, Mingming will bear the sting of disappointment when, as it goes, they sell the fuck out, even if Antares tries to tell him it was inevitable. I-CHOR would be the greatest band in the universe had they stayed where they started—a slapdash translunar studio, broadcasting from the literal dark side of the moon—but maybe becoming legible to the universe necessarily dilutes the blood of their message. Mingming resents this because he doesn't agree. Remember that.)

Either way, that day in the pits with them all, I-CHOR still made music that mattered. J Gong sings open-throated, unafraid. He rises up out of the crowd as they hoist him up. Sing along. Voices soaring.

He'd looked up, and even young, he knows he's nothing but a spec in the mass, but in that moment, he swears—

"—It's like he was looking right at me, addressing me. I still can't listen to that song without—without—" Kang Linjun, usually eloquent, falters. Mingming had watched enough archival footage by then to recognize the break in his voice. This is the only time Linjun has been real, through all the layers of time and recording.

"You know, that appearance was what broke the story to intergalactic news. That's when I knew I had to do something like him," said Linjun with a wry twist to his mouth. "It didn't *exactly* work out, but, well. I'm happy where I am."

"Please," he'd said, and wasn't sure what he was asking Jora until his face fell. "You can do something, can't you?"

Jora sighed. "This is only because I think you'd miss it."

"I would," Mingming said. "It would kill me." This life was about compromises. Mingming had seen enough to know that would have been true, regardless of his particular set of memories. Idolhood is a set of self-imposed questions: What makes it worth it? What is the reward at the end of a long stretch spent holed up in practice rooms? The bluster. The glory. Making something beautiful; making something that mattered.

"Please," he said again. "Come on, Jora, why tell me if you're not going to help?"

"Do you want to be a movie star?" The question comes out blunt.

The kid—he's approximately the same age as Mingming, of course, to make this work—pulls himself up and out of the finishing pose of his audition choreo. "What?" he asks.

"I have an offer for you," says Mingming.

This kid is shrewd, it seems. He must've been, to make it this far in the auditions—to be willing to become something else to make his dreams come true.

Linjun had been angry, the day of the fatal audition. Mingming has managed to fish this singular memory out—it'd been a recurring dream before he understood what it meant. He didn't know why it stuck until he'd gotten to the end, and then he understood completely. Narabit had asked him—what do you want? And he didn't have an answer. He recited the line they'd given him, and it was hollow. He said, I want—I want—And he was so angry at himself. What had he done with his life? I want to be great, he said. Maybe she wanted him because it was pathetic. The script was something meta, a historical set on Earth-Prime, an actor stuck in a rut after the fresh wave of AI had stolen all his roles.

But Linjun's want was without direction; Mingming had forgotten, too. What has he done with his life? He has made it so that people will listen. He is loved. I-CHOR's J Gong forgot the Belt and died a rich man's death, sedative meds bubbling in his veins. When Mingming lies in the shush of cryo, he's grateful for the chance he's been given: to remember how to shape his desire, whet it by conviction.

"Have you ever thought about what you would want, if you weren't here?" Antares asked him a year into their career. They were close—too close—and there was a nakedness to Antares' face that Mingming couldn't—still can't—stand. There were no cameras. They could have done anything they wanted.

"What do you mean?" Mingming pretended not to know what he meant.

He shifted in the dark. They were still playing small venues, not nearly big enough for a proper intergalactic tour. Their beds were still only beds, and plus, they had to share. Antares' weight drew the shitty mattress down, on his side. "Mingming," he started.

"Sorry," said Mingming. He flicked the light off, turned around.

• • •

So they play Ceres. Venus and all its terraformed beauty behind them, Mingming requested this show special, and Jora more than delivered. Hard not to believe that he's not playing favorites, a little. Ceres is nothing like the Venutian landscape—here, there are no swirling orange clouds, no stadium on stilts. The venue is small, only in the tens of thousands. It's still packed to the brim.

The atmosphere here is fucked from centuries of drilling, tinged purple at the edges and heavy with silt. Nowhere else is the sky so mottled. Mingming's breath catches in his throat. He'd forgotten this, the smoggy dense, the humid hug of landing planetside, a place where people still make things with their hands. Sol's mouth is dropped open in awe, visible underneath the edge of his respirator mask.

There's a long, long line of fans, cluttering the streets. Mingming can see them stretch back all the way to the industrial zone, thousands of waiting bodies. They'd been lining up since the early morning hours, eschewing clock-in time for this one special opportunity.

They demonstrate a simple principle: passion for passion. The alchemy of having something to say to someone who would listen. Ceres bright and bigger than it is in all their eyes, the promise of something better. The knot in Mingming's heart slackens, unravels completely. This is what he wants to do, forever.

Hovering in the wings, he takes in a full lungful of air. Out there, the crowd is waiting. It's not dark enough yet for the venue lights to be the only bright thing, so if Mingming peers out, he can see all the bobbing heads, a few last-minute stragglers like ants, trailing to their spots. Brilliant sunset ushers them forward.

Everything is bright and clear. Mingming's body is solid and real. There is urgency here, like riding a wave about to crash down. He steps out. The clouds have spread out over the audience, a soft dusting of pure color snaking between the rows. Pinpricks of light poke out through the mist. Each and every glittering point is someone here to watch him perform, breathless in the gathering dim.

Music trickles in. Mingming closes his eyes, sings full-throated, openhearted. Ceres is beautiful, and it is his. Everyone is watching him. He is the best version of himself he will ever be.

ABOUT THE AUTHOR

Em X. Liu is a Chinese diaspora writer and physician born in Tianjin and currently living between Toronto and Vancouver. Em is the 2024 Astounding

Award nominated author of *The Death I Gave Him* and *If Found, Return to Hell,* both published by Solaris Books/Rebellion Publishing.

Aktis Aeliou, or
The Machine of Margot's Destruction
NATALIA THEODORIDOU

He knows she is coming before she understands what it is she's looking for. He doesn't know her name yet—it is Margot—but when he hears it for the first time, he will think of all its meanings ("pearl" and "child of light" and "daisy"), and he will decide that only a few of those meanings suit the woman who bears it. He will wish she had a different name.

But Margot is on her way already, and this incomplete exchange of names will happen soon, because she has detected the strange heat signal and was dispatched to investigate the planet he chose to retreat to, believing it remote enough, barbarous enough to hold his grief, his excess of sight, his longing for deprivation.

On her way, in the frail craft that is slipping through the quiet dark, so little separating her from the hostilities of the universe, Margot likes to spend a few minutes every day writing in her journal. She has to write in it, of course—it is mandatory—but writing on real paper using her hand and a pen was her choice, and she enjoys the physicality of it. The movement of it and the ritual.

Her conversations with Jeff over the comms are civil but brief. She is always the one to check in at the appointed times, though it is considered good manners (if not protocol) for Control to regularly initiate contact. It makes the ones on the float feel like they're cared for, and, if humanity has learned one thing in its century of space travel, it is that there is no substitute for that connection to the ground, that tether to the soil on which a person's loved ones still roam, that umbilical cord of sanity. But Jeff has chosen to ignore all that in the face of the strain in their relationship, which used to be sexual, until it wasn't. It only proved to Margot how small a man he really is; it was his pettiness, after all, his narrow-mindedness, the aridity of his emotional landscape that drove Margot away. At her worst, though, Margot can't help but admit to herself that she'd been expecting the failure in their relationship. After all, sooner or later, everyone leaves. Leaves her. And that's not on Jeff. Can't be.

Perhaps, if she were better, someone would stick around for the long haul.

Still, Margot never expected Jeff's bitterness to spill over into unprofessionalism or, worse, negligence that could put her life in actual danger. But when her thrusters reported a malfunction on her way down to Maes-II, a time when Jeff should have been monitoring her every move, he was nowhere to be found. She ran diagnostics on her comms, fearing that she had lost contact, but all seemed to be in good working order, which should have been comforting but instead made everything slightly worse. Had Jeff received her distress call and chosen to ignore it? To avert his eyes? That would be criminal. He was an asshole, but surely he couldn't actively wish her dead. Or forget about her—he wouldn't want his own career jeopardized like this. Would he? Perhaps it was her fault. He always accused her of being overly self-sufficient. One of his main grievances against her was that she had never truly needed him. Perhaps, then, he simply thought she would be fine no matter what. Margot Lem had always been so good at everything; it was inconceivable that she might one day need his help. Even when descending for the first time, alone, on an alien, inhospitable planet.

And so her calls went unanswered.

The last thing she remembers seeing, and the first part of him—him, *Him*—she knew, was his radiance. The impossible halo, the crowned skin blazing with the brilliance of a thousand suns.

When he finds her—or, rather, when he chooses to be in her presence, for he had always known where she was, and so she had never been lost to him, nor ever would be—she is unconscious in the damaged fuselage of her craft. He notices she had the forethought and composure to get herself into her protective suit and seal her helmet before her craft lost pressure. If she hadn't, she would be dead, and this would have been a first contact of a very different kind. At least for her. Death means different things to each of them.

He had debated not coming to her rescue. After all, her arrival had been an intrusion on his much-needed, much-sought solitude. He wished not to lay eyes upon another living being for a hundred years. More. The rocks and sand and molten metals of this land were what his heart had been after. And yet, here she is. He'd always been a witness, all-seeing, all-illuminating; that had forever been his burden. He'd come here craving isolation, an averting of the eyes that was only available to him when there was nothing for him to observe. He wanted to see no more tragedy or joy, no more wanting, no more need. And yet, here she is. Here she is. No matter what the stories said of him, his shunning of loves, his affection only for the companionship of meek, bleating beasts, he'd always had a soft core.

And, for all his years of self-exile, he hasn't forgotten the rules of courtesy. He dims himself before he enters her fuselage. It is not a comfortable feeling; perhaps, the closest he's ever come to physical pain: a restraining that penetrates much more than the skin, a holding that restricts much more than breath. But he does it because he doesn't wish to hurt her. He's never wished to hurt anyone who didn't deserve it.

When she comes to, she thinks she's hallucinating. Who could blame her? She squints behind her visor, his presence still too bright for her despite all his dimming. She thinks she's dead. Transported somewhere, perhaps, a final, improbable answer to all the questions every human being everywhere, everywhen, has at one point asked. Then a pain in her chest—she must have thrashed against her restraints pretty violently on her way down—forces her to reckon with the possibility that she is not dead, and this is really happening. There is a being here with her. It is coming toward her.

She strains, tries to retreat, get as far away from it as she can. But she is still strapped to the chair. Desperately, she fumbles with the buckle, while the being raises its arms slowly and placatingly, the way she would have if she'd been approaching a wild, frightened animal.

It is hard, but she manages to slow her breath. Whatever is going to happen to her now, she has to let it. In that moment, she accepts everything that is to come. She doesn't know it yet, but this is it, now, here: she gives herself over to him—yes, him, not it. Him, *Him*. She surrenders.

He kneels next to her chair and gazes at her for a few moments. She finds it is impossible for her to look into his eyes—as if these eyes are made only to look. Not to be looked at.

Gently, he reaches out and places his hands on either side of her helmet. He pushes, then twists. Panic rises in her again as she realizes he's about to remove her helmet and suffocate her. But he is looking at her. He shouldn't be able to see her eyes behind her lowered sun visor—and yet, she's certain he is looking into them.

He twists again and lifts. Her helmet unlocks with a gasp.

She doesn't suffocate. Death doesn't come.

Slowly, painfully, she breathes.

Margot takes in her surroundings. The damage to her craft is extensive, but perhaps it's not unsalvageable. Power is still on. Comms lights are still on—not that Jeff has made any attempt to contact her or respond to her distress calls. And yet, her breathing calms further. Her heart rate approaches normal. No longer a jog by the shores of home—remember those, the early morning runs in the crisp, bird-infested air—but a leisurely walk on a balmy afternoon.

The dazzling creature in front of her is waiting for her. Patiently, she thinks.

She doesn't understand how it's possible for her to breathe. The cabin is clearly depressurized. Then, she sees it through the glass: a faint rippling just beyond the craft's exterior, like a membrane that cocoons it, and herself within it.

"Did you do this?" she asks.

He cocks his head at her. Her pulse rises again. This is not a human being, she reminds herself. He is not a man. This is first contact.

Her mind rummages inwardly for her first contact protocols, even though she knows she is well past that point. First contact took place while she was unconscious. First contact has probably already saved her life.

The being in front of her seems both humanoid enough and innocuous enough that she determines she can skip however many steps there are before trying to establish communication. She starts by telling him her name, and that she is here on a peaceful surveying mission, nothing more. She tries several other languages, including sign. She even tries singing—hastily, she chooses an Irish dirge mourning the death of a loved one at sea. Later, she will wonder at her choice.

But now, here, the being responds in English.

He says, "I have heard such songs before."

"How?" she asks.

"Margot," he says as if replying. "Your name is Margot."

"You understand me?" she asks and thinks she detects a whisper of amusement in the quirk of his lip that almost resembles a smile. And, also, some arrogance.

"Isn't it obvious I do?" he asks, the halting tone of his first words quickly falling away. His voice is smooth and, she thinks, dangerous. Like molten, precious metal. Something beautiful that can deliquesce your bones. "Are you hurt?" he asks. He knows she isn't, but he wants her to know it, too.

As if his question is an instruction, she unstraps herself and lifts herself off her chair. She checks herself, from the surface inward: bleeding—only scrapes; muscle—tight but fine; bones—intact. Is there anything else to check? Her mind, her mind. "I am fine," she says.

There is so much she wants to ask him. But he speaks again: "I should leave you in peace, to get your bearings." There is something archaic to his diction, his cadence. "I shall come back."

She thinks to protest, but she doesn't. They agree to meet again in twelve hours, after she's had a chance to rest. She watches him leave. He pierces the strange membrane that surrounds her craft without disrupting it, and then he ambles, unprotected, on the lethal-to-her surface of Maes-II. Before long, he disappears from view.

Margot inspects the damage to her craft. She thinks she can fix most of it; perhaps to the point where she won't even need to be rescued. She tries to make contact with base again, though Jeff does not respond. She talks to him anyway. Tells him: "There is a being here. Something we've never encountered before." She pauses, licks her lips. "He is magnificent," she whispers. She has no idea if her messages are getting through. She imagines Jeff on the other side, sitting in a darkened room with his arms crossed, the luminous console in front of him. "Can you hear me?"

Then, she writes about the encounter in her little paper notebook. Finds it difficult to describe him; as if the words slip from her grasp, inadequate. She closes the notebook and, huddled in her bed module, surrounded by the safety of his membrane, she sleeps.

When he comes back, she requests to use her measuring organs on him, and he—magnanimously, he thinks—allows it. Her gadgets register him—as much of him as they are capable of registering: impossible lumen, no matter how much he dims himself. Off-the-charts heat that should have reduced her and everything else around him to ash. Less than ash.

Margot knows two things, in that moment: he is the source of the strange signal that lured (did she really mean to think "lure"?) her here, and he is not what she expected to find. What did she expect? A nuclear reactor. A radioactive crater. Something devastating. Not this, not him. *Him.*

She writes down the results without comment while he watches her with his unseeable eyes. Then, Margot points at the membrane outside. "Did you make this?" she asks.

"Yes," he says. She thinks he sounds gracious. Benevolent. Understands that, if he wished, he could collapse it and kill her in an instant. She says so. Then adds: "But I trust that you won't."

"Why do you trust?" he asks.

He considers trust. Remembers all the betrayals of his youth—if he ever had such a thing as youth—small and large. A dungeon for his rays, once, and, once, the poison-dipped tip of a knife to the freshly knitted flesh above his heart. He's been wearing this bronze skin ever since.

She says, "Because life would be so diminished if I didn't."

"What a concept," he says.

"Very human, maybe," she replies.

He pauses. She appears calm, but he can hear the excited flutter of her heart. "Are you teaching me what it is to be human?" he asks.

"No," she says. "Are you learning?"

He smiles. Chooses not to speak.

"They will rescue me eventually, you know," she says.

Later, describing the end of this encounter in her notebook, she writes: *He laughs. Gilded skin, shining. For a while, I go blind.*

Again, she struggles to describe him. She wonders if this is what it was like for the bards of old, the epic poets, the mystics in their hallowed caves. She remembers the times when she was a child hiding in the closet. What was she hiding from? Nobody was looking for her.

Then, she writes: *I think he's a god.*

In their third meeting, she asks how it is he can understand her.

He considers this for some time. Finally, he speaks, and it feels to her like a concession, as if he's giving her, in that moment, more than he'd have liked: "I have wintered on the shores of a land where a version of your language was spoken."

"On Earth?" she asks because it is important, in such situations, to be as clear about one's origins as possible.

"Yes," he says. "Long ago." She notes he neglects to determine how long.

"But anyway, it is not my language," she says, surprising herself with the self-disclosure. "Just the one I use."

She can see this piques his interest. It pleases her.

"What is your language?" he asks. He puts extra emphasis on "your," as if a language can ever be something you own.

"Greek," she says.

"Ah, well," he says, and it seems to her something comes over him then, nostalgic and fierce. He recites: "ἀκτὶς ἀελίου, τὸ κάλλιστον ἑπταπύλῳ φανὲν Θήβᾳ τῶν πρότερον φάος, ἐφάνθης ποτ᾽, ὦ χρυσέας ἀμέρας βλέφαρον, Διρκαίων ὑπὲρ ῥεέθρων μολοῦσα." He trails off, as if he can't quite remember what comes next. Margot gets the sense he doesn't care to.

"It's from an old play," he says. He remembers watching it. From above, everyone looked so small, for all their efforts to seem larger than life, with their masks, their thunder devices and god machines.

"Oh," Margot replies, slightly embarrassed. "I meant modern Greek. This is ancient. I only understand fragments of it."

"Modern?" he asks. Thinks of the land he used to know. How long has it been? How much could it have changed that its language is no longer similar enough to be intelligible to its dwellers? He considers the meaning of time. Remembers dawns, dusks, a journey across the hourless curvatures of sky. He says: "I flew a chariot there, once. Over your land."

She quirks an eyebrow, though she is not surprised anymore. Still, she understands there are instructions to this theater. "Flew?" she asks.

"It's slower than it sounds," he says, his smile so dazzling it is painful to look at. "Took all day."

In her notes, later, she writes: *He has a sense of humor. For a god.*

He helps her repair her craft after that. She notes the effortless way his body moves as if neither weight nor resistance nor anything else could ever impede him in any way. The only strain she manages to detect is the one he brings upon himself, though its source and purpose remain hidden from her understanding. He makes sure they do, and it really is effort. He hasn't had to conceal himself so well and for so long in over a thousand years. At times, he wonders why he does it, but he finds he doesn't wish to know. Some things are better left as mysteries—things of the self most of all.

Margot enjoys watching him, being around him. He brings a warmth to the air that is pleasurable; she finds herself shedding her work suit in favor of T-shirts that leave her arms bare and glistening with sweat. He watches her, too. She wonders if she should feel embarrassed under his gaze, but she doesn't. It's as if she's known him all her life; or, no, that's not right. It's as if she's been known by him her entire life.

Once every twelve hours, she tries to contact Jeff but doesn't dare hope she will get through. She tells herself she has resigned to the idea that he can't possibly hear her, that no help is coming, and that she has to rescue herself. If she chooses to.

The luminous man develops the habit of lingering even after a day's work is complete, which, given the way light is mostly unchangeable in this place, only means the moment Margot is too tired to continue. He expands the membrane, then, and offers her his hand. She still doesn't know his name, but she takes his hand. He leads her outside and, together, they sit on the ground. He makes a fire; she always watches him make it but finds that afterward, no matter how hard she tries, she can never remember how he made the fire happen. She starts to think of those hours spent by the fire with him as night.

On this night, she watches him as he gazes far into the distance. The surface of the planet is gray and steely—a sharp contrast to the warm, golden hues of his skin.

"How did you get here?" she asks.

He studies her in turn. "Is this really what you want to know?" he asks, and she realizes that no. It is not.

She tries again. "When did you get here?" But once more her question falls flat and fails to ask what she means to know. She understands that time, for him, holds little weight. A different meaning.

Finally, she settles on the question that she feels will yield the most. The things she wants to know, the ways his mind works, his chest works, the heart muscle within it, if it is there at all. She figures it must, even if he has no use for it. She wishes she could take a stethoscope to him, listen for a heartbeat, ponder its rhythms. "Why did you come here?" she asks.

He considers telling her the truth. But could he ever put it into words that she could comprehend? Perhaps he could, but he chooses not to and hides instead behind his outdated grasp of her language. Besides, he tells himself, what concepts can encompass his magnitude? None, none at all. Is there any point in trying?

He senses this woman before him has a dark side, like his sister, her home planet's moon, hidden away, never touched by the light of the sun. He knows this about Margot, too: she was not an abused child, only ignored. She never felt seen by the people who ought to love her when she was young. It wasn't even malice on their part, just incompetence, just busyness and misplaced priorities. But, as children are wont to do, she found an explanation for that neglect in herself: she simply wasn't enough. Her parents were gods, they were the sun and the moon. If she were abandoned, if she were hurt, it must have been her own fault. Perhaps she didn't deserve their attention.

He sees the rest of her life, too, the hermeneutics of her suffering: she has chased her reflection in another's gaze ever since the thorn of that first pain, sought the kind of mirroring that would prove to her she can be accepted, all of her, as she truly is. Which is, of course, impossible; to be thusly encompassed is only possible in the soft membranes of the womb, before one's boundaries are brought to bear. To be so enveloped as an adult means to lose one's boundaries. Such merging of the self equals its loss. It is, then, no mystery to him that Margot has always courted death, as a child and then as a young woman. The fulfillment she wishes for is beyond reach. She's asked lovers for it, but they, of course, failed to deliver it. Because what she really wants is not simply to be loved; it is to be so fully embraced that she is obliterated.

Not even he can give her what she wants. The obliteration, yes. But not the love.

What luck to meet each other here, he thinks, which is to say, what misfortune that my needs so precisely mismatch hers!

So he lies. He tells her he was exiled. That he let down his family, failed to protect a son. Could not bear to lay eyes upon another for a thousand years. And really, does he lie? Everything he says has happened at least once. Long ago.

Margot nods. As if she understands what it is to crave solitude so complete you forget you ever existed.

He doesn't visit for a few days after that. Unable to sit still (unable is not the right word, for he is omnipotent, or close enough; so, then: unwilling), he roams this planet while making sure his light remains hidden from Margot. He can, at least, spare her the temptation she presents him with—he is made to look; he is sight—and if he knows one thing, it is this: there is no temptation more difficult to resist than being invited to simply be what you are. Do what you are. This is what love had always been for him, that seeing. He loves all he sees.

In his resistance, he hallucinates. He sees the moly plant, black-rooted, white-flowered, sprouting improbably among this planet's arid rock. He remembers the blood of the giant who pursued his daughter, back when blood could give birth to things as beautiful as a plant. His daughter? Yes, what was her name? He had a daughter, once. He had many.

And flowers, so many. A lover buried alive because of him, turned into a flower. Another also, who pined for him, turning her head as he crossed the sky so she could always face him.

He doesn't want to remember. Came here because he didn't want to see any more suffering. To be alone, sightless only because there was so little to see. How dare this mortal disturb him? Ask things of him? He could destroy her. Scorch this planet into oblivion, rid himself of her that way.

He walks, barely touching the frozen ground, the planet creaking beneath him its willingness to yield. All the time, he sees her: Margot in her chair, trying to make contact with the man Jeff (so small for her, so insignificant, so unable to give her what she wants). Then Margot, pacing the length of her ship, then Margot in her bed, dreaming of heat. Though Margot doesn't know he's watching (how could he not? This is the measure of his inability; the only one), he senses her satisfaction, for the thing she needs the most is to be seen for who she really is. And he, the god, sees her.

And I, he asks himself, what do I want? He thinks of the last time he was loved, the last time he allowed himself to touch another with all he is, that he was received the way he truly is. And he answers himself: not that. Give me the love. Spare me the ashes.

He knows other things about her, too. But he also knows that the aboutness of people needs to be inflected by narration in order to be understood.

When he sees her again, he thinks, he will ask her.

The first night of his absence, Margot dreams of the luminous man. He comes into her craft while she sleeps. It is the heat emanating from him that, in the dream, wakes her. Everything she touches is scorching hot. She sees him walking toward her, and the floor melts with his every step. Still, she doesn't run away. She approaches. He could hurt her, she knows, but he doesn't. She wants to touch him. She is so close now she can smell the searing of her hair, of her eyelashes. Her skin.

"What do you want?" he asks her. Why does he ask? Doesn't he already know?

She wakes before she has a chance to answer.

She writes it down in her notebook, where she knows he'll see.

She writes, also, that it feels as if she's lived on this planet for a long time.

Soon, she stops trying to make contact with Jeff. When she writes in her notebook about that, it takes her a few moments to remember the man's name. His face is a blur, as if she's never truly seen him, just as he's never truly seen her. Could she ever have loved him?

She thinks of home, of clean air and long walks, fresh apples plucked from a dew-sparkled tree. Ocean spray, a hot shower. She misses nothing.

Eventually, he comes back. They sit by his immemorable fire, but he doesn't ask her about her need to be seen. He inquires, instead, about the death wishes of her youth. "Why?" he asks her. "What compelled you to seek death?" He means: what compels young creatures to destroy themselves? It's been so long. He doesn't remember.

She says, "The people who were supposed to love and care for me hurt me. I learned that love and care hurt, and so, only when hurting did I ever feel safe." The logic is imperfect; and yet, he understands it.

"Nobody is coming to rescue you," he says. He doesn't tell her he is the reason behind her failure to communicate with the people at her base. It wasn't his intention, only his effect—one he chose not to alter. He sees that Margot is the kind of woman who finds comfort in hopelessness, and that hope, for her, would be the cruelest thing.

"I don't need them," she replies.

"What do you need?" he asks.

She doesn't say it, but she thinks it so loudly and so clearly the word finds its resonance within the cavities of this body he's wearing, the deepest layers of this skin. It's a feeling he knows well, that he only now admits to himself he has missed. It's been a while since he was last worshipped.

And then, a new thing happens, a new-old thing: he loses control of his person. His skin glows hot, his face blinds him with its own light.

Before his heat destroys her, he flees.

Again, he roams the planet, unseen. He does not allow himself flashbacks, that inward turning of the eye, that look toward the past. He knows the past to be the only country where his light can never reach. That is the domain of other deities, Mnemosyne, a sibling to both his parents. So he avoids memory in the form of sight as much as he can. What he allows himself is the inscriptions of it on his body, the burning in the chest, the tightness behind the eyes. People are allowed to pursue their own destruction, after all. Gods and mortals both.

His eyes can't see into the past, but the future lies before him, brightly lit as a sun-drenched road: in his mind, he walks it. Soaks in that expansive feeling in his stomach that is as if he's swallowed all that surrounds him, orbit by orbit, until he reaches the end of his future and collapses into the dwarf of his own extinction. He dwells in that imagining, that distant, longed-for time. There will be no one left, then, to remember: no songs of chariots, no chronicles of boiling oceans, no one to see, no necessary witness. His eyes will be empty, and he will finally know peace.

Until then, he must endure. Hidden or not, there is no way to escape the makings of what one is. All one can do, must do, is suffer the particular idiom of his shortcomings.

When he goes back to Margot, he asks her: "Is this really what you want?"

She doesn't need to be told what he means. "Don't you want it?" she asks back.

"Gods can't always have what they want."

"Are you teaching me what it is to be a god?"

"Only this god."

"Right. Are you teaching me?"

He doesn't tell her he killed the last creature he loved because he couldn't help himself but embrace it after a century of touchless watching. He could tell her: You will allow me to suffer so? To confirm to myself that this is all I'm good for, that this is all there is for me? My love will always bring suffering, birth flames, and when the flames are gone, I will always end up alone.

But he doesn't tell her. Gods are stubborn creatures. Whoever made them, made them imperfect.

"No," he says. "Do you want to learn?"

"I read somewhere a definition of love that said it's the terrifying realization that something other than oneself is real." She pauses, tries to look him in the eyes but, once again, finds she cannot hold his gaze, or the memory of his gaze vanishes from her mind immediately, without a trace. "Do you see me?" she asks. She means: only if you see me am I real.

(The definition of love that Margot misquoted is from Iris Murdoch's *The Sea, the Sea*. He hasn't read it.) He moves closer. "If I love you, you shall die," he says. "Do you wish to die?"

"Does anyone?" (She thinks, if she gets a chance to write about this in her notebook, she will change the ending. In this other ending, she would write: *I remember his eyes, and they were beautiful.*)

They embrace.

ABOUT THE AUTHOR

Natalia Theodoridou has published over a hundred short stories, most of them dark and queer, in magazines such as *Strange Horizons, Uncanny, Beneath Ceaseless Skies, Nightmare,* and *F&SF,* among others. He won the 2018 World Fantasy Award for Short Fiction and has been a finalist for the Nebula Award in the Novelette and Game Writing categories. Natalia holds a PhD in Media and Cultural Studies from SOAS, University of London, and is a Clarion West graduate. He was born in Greece, with roots in Georgia, Russia, and Turkey.

The Happiness Institute
ANAMARIA CURTIS

We had been three Sonderian months at the Happiness Institute when the caravan came. The labs and dormitories of the institute were still painted army gray then, and the curve of the cafeteria roof was reinforced with bombproof steel. Each of us walked with the awareness that happiness was not what this place had been built for. It felt almost like a homecoming when the trucks rolled in. We had been gathered from laboratories and mission centers all over the solar system, but we had all been raised on a stream of caravans in green and gray.

We walked out of the empty laboratory, the empty patient housing, the empty offices, to watch the warehouses go up. They were standard-issue self-building structures, meant for hometown squares and distant hills alike. We shivered at the first sight of those metal beams and shining roofs, and then, one by one, we went back inside.

None of us wanted to see the boxes being unloaded, familiar though they might have been. We all had our reasons. They sent us the inventory list, and that was enough. We trailed back to our desks, our pristine benches, our bare rooms, and we paced and paced and did not watch until the army caravan rolled out, leaving us to our dented peace.

We were as isolated then as we ever had been. We had just spent the war being told to use everything within our grasp for the cause. The new cause was finding human happiness. Our institute was a never-used military training center; our subjects were ourselves. And finally we had been given our tools.

Xela called a meeting that evening. If we had a leader, which we didn't, it was Xela. She had been an army scientist before we had all been army scientists, and she carried the choices she had made in the set of her shoulders and the tightness of her jaw.

We met in the cafeteria, and Xela sat at the head of the long rectangular table. She handed out paper and pens and asked us to say what we thought happiness might be.

Yorin, the youngest of us, had been born to war. He thought happiness might be found in order and stability, in the guarantee that the library built in the remnants of a town square would be there from one day to the next, that it would always be full of books and a study room with a broken doorknob and a port from which to download mindfilms.

Lennar, who had emerged from an army lab with no history she was willing to put her name to and who woke shivering and silent in the middle of the night, thought that happiness might be found in bringing back what was lost, in turning grief to recognition. She spoke to the rest of us fervently, her features aglow with the promise of it. So much had been studied about memory—there must be some way to live in it, if happiness in the present was truly inconceivable. If memories could be processed and purified, the past could become a rare jewel, a walk in a perfectly manipulated garden.

Then there was Alborn, who still patrolled the perimeter of the institute, though ze knew that the town a few miles off did not present a threat and that protecting us would not have been within hir control if it had. Ze thought the answer to happiness lay in narrative, in the perfect exit from the doldrum toils of the body into another reality, where the stakes could be as low or as high as one liked, where events cohered to a narrative, where who came back from war and who didn't made a kind of sense, served a purpose.

Coln thought just the opposite, that the body was the answer. That happiness was chemical, a formula to be solved. He thought that the right combination of sleep and sex and sun on skin could unlock what seemed so out of reach. He wanted to start with a lack of pain, but from that foundation he wanted to build a tower, each brick a simple pleasure.

There was more, of course, but these were the principles. Some of us spoke half-heartedly of abnegation, surrender of the self, duty toward others. But this was hard for us to listen to, harder to say. We had heard so many speeches about the greater good, about what we owed to each other, and every time this had meant more work, more violence, more grief.

After we all had our say, Xela stood up, back perfectly straight, and had her turn.

"I know little of happiness," she said, and it was clear that she had rehearsed this, that she knew exactly what she wanted to communicate. "It has not been my life's work—nor yours, I know. All I believe now is that happiness must be a departure, a clean break from what has been. I think I had principles before the war. If I did, they were broken down, whittled away piece by piece in service of destruction. I hope to find my principles again, and to build them into something strong. I cannot tell any of you what to do, but as you follow your avenues of research, I would advise that you all consider doing the same."

Xela paused, and we thought she would stop, but then she passed a hand over her eyes and brushed curling silver hair back from her face and continued. "Everything here"—she held up a paper copy of the warehouse inventory—"is poison. It cannot help us. The tools of war cannot heal its wounds.

"Our budget is limited. Our timeline is nonexistent. Do what you can, or do what you like, or do nothing at all, but don't look for answers in the warehouses."

She had said she could not give us orders, but this sounded like one. We had not been trained in disobedience.

Coln wanted to dig a pool, to plant sunflowers and melon seeds. He made good progress the first week, building planters and researching the chemical makeup of toxin-free pools on Sonder. He and Alborn took the lab's single vehicle into the town to buy seeds and reported back that the townspeople, though wary, were not unfriendly.

But it was unseasonably hot, the second week, and Coln only had a single shovel, and he wanted a pool because he thought a pool would be pleasant, not because he had any delusions about the power of hard work.

Digging a hole seemed like the kind of thing that the army might have had some reason to do. In fact, many of us had seen the evidence of it—the little red diggers burrowing into the countryside, the shallow irrigation systems dug into forced terraces, the tunnels we had been taught to avoid. With Xela tucked away in her office that afternoon, it seemed such a small thing to open the inventory list and check.

Coln found the self-starting digger in the second row of the first warehouse. There was an image of it on the box, and when he crouched there on the dirt floor and put his hand to it, it opened smoothly, like it had been waiting for us to discover it.

"Look," he said to the empty warehouse. "Look how easy it is."

Lennar found the emotargeters a few days after that. She carried the boxes she found to the laboratory office that Xela never went near and wept neat, silent tears over the specs as they loaded onto her computer screen.

She could not bring anyone back to life. She could not dive into memory and live there. But the military had made this targeter to connect any one person's mind to another. To create a whole where there had been only lonely fragments.

Lennar had been a military scientist before she was ever a happiness researcher. She saw the data on her screen as clear as the rest of it—compulsion, manipulation, camaraderie coating the violence. If everything the targeter touched created connection, how easy it would be to nudge someone into an action, into an atrocity—how easy to claim it was for the greater good. She pulled one of the targeters out and examined the pieces: two silver studs to go at the back of the neck, a matching bracelet for the nondominant hand. Simple enough to install on oneself. Elegant, in their way.

She left the targeters in the box in the office, hands shaking.

Alborn walked the perimeter of the institute day by day and tried to think of stories that would make people happy. Ze saw the progress the digger made on the pool, and the garden plot, and the sandpit that Coln installed. Ze watched Lennar carry boxes up to the laboratory offices and come back down tear-streaked and empty-handed. These were not parts of a story that would make people happy.

Alborn didn't want to write about war, but any story ze tried to write without it—stories about friends, about grand declarations of love, about whole, unsullied planets where adventurers marched across countrysides—fell flat, lacked dimension. There was a dark, unseen shadow behind them, in them, always.

Alborn began to wonder if perhaps no one story could hold happiness. Ze went back to hir computer and looked at the inventory. There was a speechwriting program somewhere. Even better, there was training software, simulations. Here was a base for narrative! Branching paths, tailor-made to each user. It had been used, ze knew, for recruitment for dangerous missions and posts in remote prisons where the kind of work one did could not be spoken of. It would be a triumph, Alborn thought, to turn the simulations to a new purpose: to edit out the war, to transplant the heart. Ze would build new stories, where people had different choices and everyone had a home.

As we became familiar with the first few warehouses, we began to shrink away from Xela. It was not that she chastised us for ignoring her advice, or her orders, whichever they were. But the specter of her disapproval still dogged us. We tried to bend the tools from the warehouses to our visions, but we did it out of sight when we could. Alone, when we could. Xela must have known—for all the time she spent on her books and her notes, she still had her powers of observation—but we still avoided inevitable confrontation. It is hard to say now whether it was fear of battle or the weakness of burgeoning disobedience that kept us away from her. Perhaps it was simple dislike.

Yorin came back from town with a six-legged dog and named her Patsy. We all loved Yorin, wanted him to be the optimist, the one who looked at our world and saw a future worth shaping, and this love extended to Patsy. We fed her and patted her with hands turned suddenly clumsy in the presence of soft fur and warm brown eyes and let her sleep in whichever bed she chose.

Even Xela liked Patsy. Even Xela slipped her extra treats at the end of each meal.

Coln was still trying to figure out some of the draining and tubal systems for the pool, so he was learning to cook in the meantime. When he cooked, we all ate together.

To most of us, it felt like a detente. We had made our decisions. We each had our own projects, which we pursued as we could and dropped in order to talk over dinner. But we were still so fractured. Lennar still woke in the middle of the night and clutched the sheets until her knuckles turned white, still felt like she was the only person in the world who wasn't understood.

Alborn still followed the winding path of the training simulation, trying to tear out the core of it, to remake and reorient it toward happiness and away from misery.

And Xela read her books and watched us and said little. We watched her right back, when we felt bold enough, and wondered what principles she was building, how they might be used against us. That was all principles could be used for, as far as we knew.

The day Coln figured out the water system for the pool, Lennar put in the targeter, inserted the studs in the back of her neck in front of a mirror, her hands still slick with bathroom soap.

Nobody else was connected to it. She was just as alone. But when she woke up in the middle of the night, her mind blank and horrifyingly vast, she could touch the silver dots at the back of her neck, could run her fingers over the silver bracelet that had sunk itself into her wrist, and know that there was something other than herself living in her skin.

• • •

We were all there when Xela first noticed the bracelet on Lennar's arm. Coln had cooked, so we had eaten together, and Lennar was seated just to Xela's left.

There was butter to go with Coln's pora seed bread—an indulgence, which we were coming to appreciate meant happiness, sometimes—and Xela asked for the butter plate after a second slice of bread.

"Sure," Lennar said, passing it to her. "Here you g—"

The butter plate fell out of Xela's hand, landing with a definitive crack on the hard plastic table. Xela didn't look at it. She only looked at Lennar's wrist.

"Turn around," she said.

"What?"

Xela spoke quietly, but the command was clear. "Turn around."

The rest of us watched Lennar turn, watched Xela's eyes zero in on Lennar's neck, watched her face go still and hard.

"Thank you," she said. She reached an arm toward Lennar's neck and had nearly grasped one of the studs when Lennar finally jerked away.

Alborn was the first to approach Lennar that evening, the first to ask what the bracelet was. Ze listened quietly and solemnly as Lennar explained what the targeter did, the fact that it was meant to be one part of a multifaceted web but that she was, despite that, still alone.

"There's bad to it," she said. "I'm sure they used it for awful things, during the war."

"Everyone was used for awful things during the war," Alborn said, and it was clear ze believed it. "There is no blank page."

"Not even in a story?" Lennar asked.

"Not even then." Alborn hesitated. "I thought that if everyone had their own story to build, something that could shift and change with them, maybe they would never be really lonely again. They would feel understood."

Lennar looked down at her hands, at the glinting silver on her wrist. "You know, there's more than one way to be understood."

Alborn looked at it too. "It could be a story for everyone."

Lennar gave Alborn the bracelet, then inserted the first metal stud into the back of hir neck, so carefully. With the second, she was less careful, and she winced with Alborn as it went in, then, feeling the wince, laughed. Alborn laughed too, and then they didn't stop laughing, caught in a spiral of delight.

• • •

Alborn and Lennar were happy. We could all see it, even if we couldn't feel it. And Alborn turned back to hir simulations and gave us a trial one evening, after Xela had withdrawn.

"It's not much," ze said, but it was.

We each had a different setting in the simulation, a different starting point. It was only the beginning of a story, a background, a world, but each of us, in our way, felt the undercurrent. There was something beneath the story, built into the story, pushing and pulling us toward something. When the simulations ended, we turned toward Alborn, hungry for more.

More was in the bathroom outside the recreation room, where Lennar had the studs laid out in even lines.

We filed into the bathroom one by one and let Lennar put the studs in our necks. We clasped the bracelets around our wrists ourselves.

And when Lennar woke in the early hours of the morning, we were there. The pain and fear spiked us all awake, but it wasn't so much, spread out between us. We were so sleepy. When Lennar put a finger to the cool silver of her bracelet, the rest of us felt the touch.

Xela looked at us all the next morning, and we sent reassurance among and between ourselves. There was betrayal in her look, but we did not have to feel it. We had each other, and she had nothing.

We had treated the fourth warehouse with a certain wariness, as its inventory had been vague, but the dream of the pool broke through this last barrier as it had broken through the first.

Coln thought the warehouse might house a package of the last chemical he needed, which would otherwise necessitate a wait of many weeks if not months. Everything else was in place: the tubes clear and clean, the lining pristine, the safety markings stark against the pale walls. The water was just waiting to be pumped in.

Yorin was out at the table that had been set up by the pool, scratching Patsy behind the ears, just where she liked it. He still thought that happiness might lie in stability, but he was beginning to come around to some of Coln's points about small personal pleasures—petting a dog foremost among them.

"Yorin!" Coln called. "Come help me look for the boxes of chemicals."

The sun was gentle on Yorin's head, and Patsy's fur was soft. "I don't want to," Yorin said.

"Oh, come on," Coln said. It was hotter in the warehouse. He was impatient, so close to what he'd been working toward for weeks. When he said something to Yorin, he meant it to be listened to. "It won't take long. Come help."

Did the rest of us feel it? It's hard to say. We were so new to togetherness. Regardless, Yorin went.

He went into the fourth warehouse, where it was hot and unpleasant, where the boxes weren't labeled very carefully. And he opened a crate because he had a good feeling about that one. Or because Coln had a good feeling about that one. It's so hard to say.

The crate was splintered and hard to handle. Yorin took the hem of his shirt to protect his hands, to open it with, and it halted the movement of his arm, which meant that he swung the lid of the crate only halfway off, so that the corner of it fell hard into the contents.

The explosion brought us all to our knees.

Apparently, they didn't hear it in town, but we *felt* it, searing through our minds as we buckled under the pain, wherever we were—our offices, our desks, the laboratory bench. If we had been able to think we might have rejoiced in the pain, for it meant that Yorin was still alive, to be in pain, but we could not manage even that.

It was Xela who went to pull him out of the warehouse, which was only a little dented. It had been built to withstand such explosions. When we looked at it later, we could hardly believe how contained it really had been because the pain of it was so total, so all-encompassing and overwhelming. And so we were all paralyzed by it, and it was Xela who tended to his shoulder and called the doctor from the town.

And yet.

And yet, when Yorin woke up, mind hazy, who did he turn to? Us, who siphoned off the pain, who took turns sitting next to him, our hands on his arm, palms over his bracelet. When he screamed in the night, we were there. Coln made Yorin's favorite meals, and Lennar figured out how to tweak the pain nerves in his shoulders to function a little less. Patsy lay on the foot of the bed and licked at the blankets every time Yorin moved his legs, and Alborn told Yorin everything he wanted to hear—what the sky looked like outside, what Yorin would look like when the bandages came off, that he would never be in pain and alone again.

Xela came by in the moments we least expected her, tiptoeing in to offer Yorin a snack, or a book, or an ice pack. They were well-meant attempts, we knew, but they were shadows of what we could give him. She seemed to know it, too; when she greeted us, she looked at the bands on our wrists and the studs in our necks with something like resignation instead of the disgust we had become accustomed to.

• • •

The chemicals for the pool were never found in the warehouse, but they did arrive some weeks later, as soon as we could possibly have expected them.

Coln finally pumped in the water just as the days were starting to get truly hot. We set up padded benches under army tents by the side of the pool. We plucked some of Coln's flowers to put in Yorin's hair when he came to sit at the edge of the pool and dipped his feet in. There were fresh herbs for Coln's dinners, and we all passed Yorin the best tidbits first.

Coln more than anyone doted over Yorin. Formally, it wasn't an apology. But then, who could say what had really happened? None of us truly understood the connection we had. We were all reaching out to each other—apologetic, grateful, loving, occasionally resentful—still trying to find the edges of ourselves and each other.

When one of us passed by Xela's office one evening, we saw that she had searched other bases on Sonder, somewhere she could transfer to. There were scribbled charts and notes on her desk, a photo of all of us from the first night we'd arrived at the base set as her computer background. We weren't pleased at the thought that she might leave, but we understood it. It made sense. We had each other, and she had only her principles.

We imagined her lonely, when we thought of her at all.

What we began to find was that when Yorin was pleased, it magnified. When Yorin's pain was less, so was ours.

Lennar began to sleep through the night.

Yorin took off the bandages on his shoulder on a hot day near the end of summer. Finally, he could dunk his head in the pool, and that spread through all of us just like the explosion had—this time it was a balm, cool relief.

We can't resist the call. We descend on the pool in our swimsuits and our lab coats, whatever we're wearing the moment the feeling hits. The digger was dutiful and expansive; there is room for all of us in the water.

Perhaps the enormity of it, or the ridiculousness, is why we don't notice her at first. We are busy asking Alborn to tell us a story, a group story, watching Lennar execute her perfect dive into the deep end, congratulating Yorin on the continued movement of his rotator cuff.

In this moment, the sun is hot, and the water is cool, and we are all together, basking in it. When we try to think of them, loneliness and uncertainty are distant, inaccessible memories, soon laughed off under the ruddy haze of the sun and the feeling surrounding us, created by us. It feels good, and it is good, and it will be good, if only we can stay together.

And now we see Xela, her hesitance tangible in the sting in our own throats, in the way she kneels to trail her hands in the shallow water near the stairs, silver flashing on her wrist.

She gives us hesitance; we reflect back joy. We feel her fear, her anxiety, her dismay at giving in, her relief at finally not being alone. We give her back welcome, satisfaction, certainty. There are no tides in our little pool, no currents, but there is a pull to it all the same.

Xela steps into the pool, and we all feel the relief of the water anew, pleasure reflecting pleasure. "Is this happiness?" she asks us, and there is a waver, almost a hesitation.

"Come," we tell her. We pull her deeper.

We have our answer. We need not doubt.

ABOUT THE AUTHOR

AnaMaria Curtis is from the part of Illinois that is very much not Chicago. She's the winner of the LeVar Burton Reads Origins & Encounters Writing Contest and the 2019 Dell Magazines Award, and her work has been published in magazines including *Strange Horizons*, *Uncanny*, and *Beneath Ceaseless Skies*. In her free time, AnaMaria enjoys starting fights about 19th century British literature and getting distracted by dogs.

Born Outside
POLENTH BLAKE

"You were all too young to remember this," says the teacher.

I remember everything that's ever happened to me, but I can't say things like that. Instead, I stare at the teacher's forbidden cupboard, where she keeps all the new pencils and pens. I try to peek inside sometimes, but she says no children allowed. I might take too many pencils and waste them.

"This can be upsetting, but you need to know."

The whole class is about the same age, so we were all babies then. Though Jenny was already seven over the holidays, and I won't be seven until next week. My best friend Tom is the youngest every year, so will be six almost forever, then seven when we're all eight. Peter died last month, so is six for actually ever.

"What did I just say, Tulip?"

There are times when I don't feel like Tulip at all, and I wish people wouldn't use my name, but I can't say that either, so I answer, "The pod war was the most important war in human history," because I remember even when I'm not paying attention.

She carries on the lesson and puts on a documentary about the war. I look at the walls, but the sides of my eyes will still see.

The classroom has walls in two shades of gray. Dark gray at the bottom and light at the top. They stopped using colors, as the pod people are drawn to them. Our uniforms are also designed to hide us. Gray and plastic. Nothing a pod person likes.

The video people have found the pods, and they're curious at first.

Tulips are very colorful, but that's okay. The plants saved people. My aunt lived in a poor area where the weeds grew everywhere on the paths and the pods had to fight the weeds first. They couldn't just grow out of the roads, like they did in the big cities, with nothing to stop them.

The pods are burning. I hear the screams.

My first memory was cold, but not in a bad way. My pod held me close, and I was the most Tulip I've ever been. When it opened, I saw stars twinkling through the trees in so many colors.

There were brambles close to the pod, but they weren't attacking. My aunt says they'd hidden the pod, only pulling back after she heard a baby and came near. I didn't see any of that. I just saw the thorns and thought they were pretty.

My pod kept still as she approached, let her lift me out. Once I was removed, my pod shriveled.

I cried, and my aunt comforted me.

"Tulip is very sensitive about fire," says my aunt, after they call her because I ran out crying.

My aunt is also sensitive about fire. The pods came at night. She only had her nightie and nothing on her feet, carrying my cousin Tulip. The pods pulled Tulip from her arms, but they couldn't get my aunt. The brambles were too thick, like they'd grown overnight too, and they dragged the pods down. She could have got cousin Tulip back after that, if it weren't for the people with flamethrowers, who stopped her clawing at the brambles and said they'd burn her too if she didn't run.

"How are you?" she asks me.

I scratch at my sleeves because my arms are getting itchy in the uniform that isn't for pod people. I wish I could say that I don't feel very Tulip today.

"I'm okay," I say.

"People don't understand," says my aunt as she drives us home.

"I know," I say. "I know not to tell them."

People knew that my aunt lost her baby and found one. She never told them where she found me though. Said the pods must have got my parents, but I was hidden in a fridge.

I wasn't a copy of cousin Tulip. I wasn't really a copy of anyone, not in that way. The first pod people were, but as the pods grabbed more people, they knew enough to make new people.

There was a scientist in the video who tried to say that. It wasn't what people thought, not by the end. The pods stopped fighting once everyone had scratches. The pod people never really fought, just wandered, confused, as the fire came towards them. So I cried, but also I'm glad the scientist was there.

"I can ask for you to skip history," she continues.

I keep looking out the car window, as I don't know if I want to talk about it.

"I'm okay," I repeat.

Most people aren't okay. Some people say that's because of the pod scratches. That's why there are so few babies because the scratches came with something. I think it's because they burnt all the pods with the babies.

My pod left things in my head, and I can't forget them, but I don't always remember them until I dream.

The people in charge blamed it on the rockets. They went up into space, and they brought things back. I think they're right, but it wasn't the pods. I have dreams sometimes where the pods are in space because they don't need rockets. They follow the rockets because there's something on board that isn't people.

It's pretty in space. The colors show up better. I wish I didn't have to follow the rockets. Just stay in space forever.

My aunt brings me breakfast in bed, as I have today off school. Jenny went down with the sickness, and she probably won't make it. We get the day off, so it doesn't spread, but it doesn't work like that. This isn't a sickness that spreads, not now. This is damage from the sickness that did, back when we were babies.

"How are you feeling?" she asks.

Our house is a rainbow inside. My room is yellow, and my aunt's is purple. My breakfast eggs are bright orange in the middle, and the broccoli is green. It turns out human people like bright colors as well, when they don't think the pods can see.

"A lot more Tulip," I say because nobody can hear us at home.

She smiles. "In what way?"

I read a book at the library and the librarian was surprised because it was a big book. There are hybrid tulips. They're bright and flower early. They were named after that Darwin man, who knew a lot about species.

"When I grow up, I want to be an evolutionary biologist."

My aunt looks confused, but not like she's worried that I'll hurt people. It wasn't a pod people thing to be an evolutionary biologist. It was a gifted child thing, where the teacher says I see the world in a different way, and

I'm really very smart. There have been human people who never forget, so I'm just on the edges, not totally something else.

"Life is very important," she says, as though agreeing, but she means I shouldn't turn into a pod and murder people. I understand. I wouldn't like that either.

I'm following a rocket as it passes Mars. The teacher says it's red, but it's not that simple. It's red, orange, peach, black, and white. It even looks green in the shadows, not from plants, but just the light. I wonder if the rocket people live here. I also know they don't. I'm a pod dreaming and also Tulip.

The rocket explodes.

I wake up screaming.

My aunt comes running.

"Jenny's dead," I say.

"I'm so sorry," she replies.

It wasn't as sad as it could be. Jenny could have died as a baby, like cousin Tulip. Jenny got to live and be bored in class and paint pictures of her cat for as long as she could.

I sit with Tom on a wall at the edge of the playground, scratching at my arms. The others are sick, but it doesn't usually show. They cough sometimes, then run off again, like it was nothing. They were all too young to remember what it was like to be healthy.

That's how we figured it out, that we were both born outside. We've never been sick, and we never forget.

"They're dying," says Tom.

"It was on the rockets," I say.

Tom doesn't know as much as me because he's from the first wave, even though he was born later. A pod grabbed first Tom from the cradle and started to grow my best friend Tom behind the garden shed. Keeping down, taking it slow because there were people with flamethrowers. When things settled and Tom's family found his pod, I was already born. That means I like thorns and have space dreams, and Tom remembers how first Tom loved the sound of paper.

"Do you want to come to my birthday party?" I ask.

"Will there be cake?"

"Yes, it's chocolate."

I'm the brambles in my dream, but not only the brambles. There's trees and there's mushrooms and the whole forest talks. They're not happy with the pods.

"You're hurting them," I say as the forest.

"We're saving them," I say as the pods.

It goes around and around, but the brambles end up a bit pod and the pods a bit bramble. That's why the first pods grabbed, and the later ones scratched. They knew life was important before, but only in general. They didn't understand that one baby mattered.

The others run around at my party. It's in the garden and a few get scratches from the brambles.

My aunt lets the brambles do what they like on the fences because they saved her and protected my pod. She only picks at them when the flowers are odd colors and the blackberries look like tiny pods, because otherwise the people with flamethrowers will be back, and we're all sensitive about fire.

"Do you think they'll die?" says Tom, through a mouthful of cake.

"Not yet," I say.

My aunt hears us and is concerned.

"Don't worry, the scratches will delay it," I say. "Life is important."

I tie my laces in a loose knot, so they come undone during class. The rest head out to the playground with the teacher as I tie my laces back up. As soon as she's out of sight, I head to the forbidden cupboard and pull the doors open.

There are stacks of boxes with pencils and pens. Even the fancy, colored ones we use for special projects. There are rolls of star stickers saying how good we've been. The only thing that isn't for us is the scissors with the points at the end, as only the teacher gets to use those.

"Did you find what you expected?" asks the teacher, back from showing the others out.

I know I've missed something that doesn't want to be seen. Something that keeps drawing me to the cupboard. I look harder. There are pots of paper clips, and pins, and seeds, and paper fasteners.

"What are those seeds?" I ask.

She's scared, and nobody should be scared when I'm only seven.

"I like plants," I say. "I'm going to be an evolutionary biologist."

She picks up the seed pot. "When each student ends up in hospital, I take a seed for them to hold and make a wish. These ones hold the wishes."

That sounds sad, but also, I don't think so because those seeds are for pods. I've only seen them in my dreams before now because the flamethrowers got them all.

"I wish they could grow," I say.

She studies me and then takes some seeds from the pot. She hands them to me.

"When you're older," she says like she thinks I will be for sure, with all the others slowly dying. "Only when you're older."

I nod because I understand. She's worried the flamethrower people will find her seeds. She was also born outside.

There's a bit of Peter and Jenny in the seeds, and a bit of all the others, saved before they died. Their babies will be born outside and be safe from what the rockets brought home.

I'll make my own seeds when I'm older, but I'm not my pod. I won't die, and my babies won't burn, because we'll be all that's left in the end. But until then, the rest will be scratched because life is important.

I tell Tom all this.

"Do you believe me?" I ask.

He picks at the sleeve of his uniform. "I don't like hiding."

"It's bad plastic," I say. "My aunt has a cotton cushion, and it's the best, and we can all wear cotton again."

"Can we wear colors?" he asks.

I nod. "Really bright ones."

My aunt is in the kitchen making us sandwiches. She's coughing.

"She's dying," says Tom.

"I know," I say. "But we'll give her as long as we can."

Tom doesn't understand yet because he's going to be six for almost ever, but now that I'm seven, the itching has stopped, and my thorns have grown under my sleeves. Hybrid tulips bloom early with all the colors, and I'll grow up to be an evolutionary biologist who doesn't have to hide.

I want to be happy about that, but I think about cousin Tulip and first Tom, who died to flamethrowers and pods not understanding. I wish they could wear colors too.

I dream that I'm in the garden. The brambles grow around my feet, and the stars shine in their colors on my bare arms. My thorns are too big to be covered, but I've painted the tips in yellow and purple. For the first time since my pod opened, I'm completely Tulip.

ABOUT THE AUTHOR

Polenth Blake lives in England with a menagerie of invertebrates. They've previously had work in *Strange Horizons*, *Nature*, and the *Rosalind's Siblings* anthology.

Hive Minds and Drones: Bees Earthside in Futuristic Tech and Science Fiction

D.A. XIAOLIN SPIRES

Honeybees make a surplus of honey. As it turns out, honey is not only sweet and tasty, but also imbued with so much meaning in the English language and beyond: a term of endearment, symbols of prosperity and abundance (as in "the land of milk and honey" with biblical and religious intonations), and starry-eyed intervals after marriage (honeymoons). Honey is the sweetest animal-excreted liquid but leave it on the counter or in the pantry months too long, and it also turns into a crystal.

Humans have been extracting honey for quite a long while, with rock paintings from Spain as early as the Mesolithic period, dating from around 8000 BCE to 2000 BCE, depicting early honey hunting as an opportunistic means by nomadic hunters and gatherers. These rock paintings feature animal figures grouped around humans, including the earliest depiction of a ladder made of ropes and sticks used in the process of honey gathering.

Likewise, archeological evidence of honey consumption in China goes back to the seventh millennium BCE. Under chemical analysis, pottery jars from the Neolithic Henan Province in China reveal the existence of what was a honey, rice, and fruit-fermented drink from that period. Additionally, the earliest written record in China of bees or beelike entities was Feng 蜂 (or the ancient equivalent of this modern word), the Chinese character for bee/wasp was inscribed in animal bones dated to about three thousand years ago.

The ancient counterpart to the modern character honey, Mi 蜜, was recorded later in 300 BCE in the *Book of Rites*, one of the Confucian

Five Classics that discusses developing character and propriety. Honey in the Confucian context was mentioned for consumption as a dietary recommendation.

In terms of apiculture, records of beekeeping came later, in Yuan dynasty agricultural manuals, and hive-keeping was a common practice during the imperial period of China. A scholar who kept bees in the mid-second century CE was mentioned in a third century CE text in ancient China.

In ancient Rome, honey was used in a recipe for Punic or Phoenician porridge, that included cheese, groats (milled grains), and honey as ingredients. Pottery in West Africa also shows early use of honey, which dates back to three thousand and five hundred years ago. It's also worth noting that a team of scientists studied four hundred and fifty prehistoric broken pieces of ceramic from the Central Nigerian Nok culture and found beeswax, which arises from processes of wax comb-melting or honey storage and cooking.

Honey was important as a means of preserving food in ancient times given its high sugar (monosaccharides fructose and glucose) concentration. People took advantage of how honey acts as an antibacterial by immersing their food in honey. This golden viscous substance made of the labor of bees induces water out of yeast and bacteria through osmosis and endows food with a longer shelf life. Not to mention the caloric value of honey and appealing sweet taste that has people risking getting stung to gain access to the lovely liquid.

And bees, well, they are busy, no matter if we are talking about our past or our present! They have much work to do, including rolling out stunning architectural feats, pollinating, and making that sweet treacle. As a corollary to my recent *article on bees in space*, which discusses real space bee organisms and technology and science fiction counterparts, this article discusses recent terrestrial technological feats involving bees, many related to the procurement of honey, as well as bees in science fiction based on futuristic Earth.

Artificial Bees and Bee-Inspired Tech on Earth

Honeybees face many interrelated threats including poor nutrition, parasites, pathogens, and pesticides. Additionally, in apiculture, bee-keepers face industries like almond pollination, which are heavy hitters in regard to their aggressive use of bee colonies. Colony Collapse Disorder (CCD) has also been an ongoing issue contributing to the devastation, first reported in 2006–2007, though earlier phenomena not such named existed.

CCD occurs when the majority of worker bees disappear in a hive, leaving the queen, nurse bees, and a brood of immature bees behind. Without that essential structure to tend to the hive, the colony goes kaput. To compensate for the loss, commercial beekeepers must split hives, buy queens, and create more colonies.

To deal with these ongoing threats, companies and researchers have designed everything from artificial bees to help with pollination to state-of-the-art hives.

Do you need a little bee-sized drone with lights and horse hairs? Enter Eijiro Miyako, a researcher at Japan's National Institute of Advanced Industrial Science and Technology. He uses a specialized ionic liquid gel to collect and transfer pollen repeatedly without compromising the health of pollinators, making it biocompatible and eco-friendly. The number of drones needed to replace colonies, though, would be staggering. Also inspired by *Apis mellifera*, Wyss Institute at Harvard's RoboBees are another smart insect intended for agriculture or disaster relief.

Are you worried about the sesame-sized mite that burrows into your abdomen? Well, meet the smart home of your dreams! The whimsically named HIVEOPOLIS has integrated Internet, satellite data, and robots. Nervous about the bloodsucking Varroa mite infestation or flowers with pesticides? No worries, the built-in vibrating plates will deter you! Want to know where to get food? A dance robot will do the latest jig to show you to sources of pollen and nectar. Not sure where to have your hive? Don't worry, HIVEOPOLIS will have you back in, mapping out the best spots for grabbing your yummy pollen/nectar "grub." Need to be inspected before proceeding? Here at HIVEOPOLIS, we have double doors and blasts of air to keep you in place. Worried about bad weather? HIVEOPOLIS has meteorological services, too, connecting colonies to necessary data.

Although I'm using a rather tour and sales-guidey tone to embody the voice of HIVEOPOLIS' ambitions, I'm not intending to be flippant or cheeky here. HIVEOPOLIS really does boast about doing these things. Social cooperation isn't just among the bees, but in the HIVEOPOLIS ethos, which also includes humans, robots, and their living environments. It's not a taking over of bees by artificial bees, but a truly cooperative living, learning, and hive experience.

Lastly, in Australia, the last continent standing free of the varroa mites, a team of engineers who worked on the Mars rover employed their skills and designed a striking purple beehive. Aptly named "The Purple Hive Project," the hive uses AI and high-def cameras to sense parasitic mites. Offering this new technology to ports, which are often susceptible to foreign invasive entities, the eventual goal is that the purple hive can be attached to any beehive to create a "mesh network" in Australia. The team has already positioned one hive at the Townville port, with entering bees going through what looks like airport security, where they are scanned (for mites) at gate entry. If the bee is found to host the offending pest, an SMS message gets sent to authorities, and the bee is contained for inspection.

Humans and Aliens as Bees: Hives and Hive Minds

Switching gears, let's talk sci-fi, inspired by our Terran pollinators and honey-makers. In terms of shared perceptions, hives—as in hive minds—are a trope in science fiction, useful in thinking about alternate consciousnesses.

For example, let's consider the novelette "The Beekeeper" by Wang Jinkang, published in Chinese. The novelette opens on the potential murder of a research assistant. Adding to the mystery of the moment, the bewildering sentence, "The beekeeper's edict: do not wake the bees" is the only thing left on a nearby computer screen.

Numerous questions build throughout the story as to whether bees have knowledge of activities imposed upon them by humans, including breeding, being transported, colony and all, to sources of nectar and extraction of the bees' hard-earned honey.

Wang also presents an interrelated greater question about critical mass: can we relate collective bee intelligence to the possibility of a kind of superintelligence of computers and networks? In this eerie, enigmatic mystery, the story ultimately offers up the idea of the hive mind as networked, as related to the higher functions of neurons in brains or the technological progress of networked computers beyond critical mass.

Sci-Fi Humans-Turned-Bees: Physiology

Like Jupiter Ascending's half-human and half-bee Stinger Apini featured in the abovementioned article on space bees, Liuli of the Chinese anime "B.E.E" (streamed also in Japanese and issued in episodes of fifteen-minute increments) is also a part-human, part-bee superhuman, crafted through bioengineering. She must use her bee-drawn skills to execute some high-stakes hostage rescuing.

Mechanical Drones and Cooperation

In "How Bees Fly" by Simone Heller, the reader gets the feeling that there is something amiss with the narrator, Salpe's, community. Salpe, the midwife protagonist, makes contact with "demons" and is exiled from her community to live with those who have contaminated her. These demons appear "like decent people to [her]"—at first glance, they are no different from other travelers until you look closer, at the eyes, which are white, and their skin, smooth and soft.

Salpe finds out they give birth to live creatures rather than lay eggs. Eventual details give the reader evidence to think, "Hey, maybe it's the protagonist's (ex-)community that is the one that departs more from human life and is more like bees," at least in biological traits.

The species of the protagonist hatch from eggs . . . and we later learn, may have stings (whether that line is used metaphorically is unclear, but suggests a physiological appendage). While most details suggest that the strange beelike beings are the members of the Society, there is one social, rather than physiological, aspect of the demons that is portrayed to be like in-real-life bees. Salpe discovers that the demons also dance, in joy (just as bees do on our in-real-life Earth).

Bees, little insecty ones, like ones on Earth, also exist in this fictional world. Beehives make an appearance, too. Dead bees are the first bees the readers encounter, which the midwife collects on her way back from the unexpected meeting with the demons, as the midwife tends to the beehives, grounding the hives in storms and helping the bees reproduce. Salpe's (ex-)community extracts juice from beehives, much like how in-real-life humans collect bee honey. The dead bees portend the bad news of Salpe's exile, but perhaps also some greater injustice.

It turns out the bees the midwife tends to are mechanical, but that doesn't make them any less lovable. It just makes them resilient after presumed death. Bees here are literal, as machine drones first presumed organic, but they are also metaphorical, allegorical devices toward achieving clarity.

To know how bees fly in this story is to understand who has deeper knowledge about the world about them, i.e., the revivable machine physiology that populates the hives—and more importantly, to consort with the enemy and see their humanity, perhaps literally—and to be resurrected like a machine bee into a more enlightened state. Bees here are physiological, mechanical, drones in both the technological and zoological sense, providers of nutrients but also makeshift weaponry. They are resources, companions, and wellsprings of greater truths about humanity and monsterhood.

Mechanical drones, too, in the shape of bees make an appearance in "The Artificial Bees" by Simon Guerrier, in an environment with all fauna death, and leaving only flora behind. They sting to protect nectar from outside threats, which includes at least one human. The characters in the story speculate about whether the bees realize they are not alive but ultimately, they believe it's better for the machine bees not to know. The story embraces these mechanical bees in the discussion of loftier and sorrowful matters of life, death, and species extinction, as well as what it means to be a machine drone, zipping from flower to flower.

In my story, "The Queen of Calligraphic Susurrations" the main character is a beekeeper of mechanical drones and finds it hard to produce writing automatically like the bees do with honey, drawing from ideas of labor, automation, authorship, and fabrication. The sound of these drone bees buzzing resonates with another phantom sound made by a generative AI in action that draws from her biological data.

Beestings on Earth

"The Weapons of Wonderland" by Thoraiya Dyer, a short story in epistolary form written by a vet, starts out with beestings and two women hoping to save a planet in doom (and their "birds and the bees"!).

They attempt to achieve this through grand technological enterprises, such as gathering DNA from placental mammals to make a biblical-inspired Noah's Ark and enhancing Earth's life with the comet Wonderland's resilient and transformative creatures: rabbits, unicorns, caterpillars, and oysters that can adapt to many environments through their metamorphic abilities.

Other animals, such as rabbits, make more of an appearance than bees, but bees do catapult the story into action with their stings and vulnerability, and they showcase Alya's (one of the characters) interest in protecting them. One can't help but think of colony collapse in our real-life Earth environments and the devastation this might cascade in these tightly woven ecological networks. (See Maja Lunde's novel, *The History of Bees*, for a look at futuristic ecological devastation in relation to bees and beekeeping spanning from England in 1852 to China in 2098.)

"At the Mouth of the River of Bees" by Kij Johnson deals with road trips, Montana, and—rather intimidatingly—large bee migrations, formed into a river of bees. The first line of the story is "it starts with a beesting . . . " and catapults into an evocative, sensory-rich journey that culminates in meeting the literal queen bee.

Beyond Fiction

Like *Apiary*, which features bees in space, board games like *Honey Buzz*, *The Bears and the Bees*, and *Hive*, also allow humans to encounter and play as their charming insect counterparts. It's a way for humans to be bees, if only for a post-meal evening.

Bees have been so intertwined with human history, and especially in the agricultural sector of beekeeping for honey. Science fiction provides us an outlet to envision futuristic bees, human-bee identities, and swarms of sentience—and let their captivating buzzing and delicious honey linger in our (hive or non-hive) minds.

ABOUT THE AUTHOR

D.A. Xiaolin Spires steps into portals and reappears in sites such as Hawai'i, NY, various parts of Asia and elsewhere, with her keyboard appendage attached. Her work appears in publications such as *Clarkesworld, Analog, Nature, Terraform, Fireside, Star*Line, Liquid Imagination,* and anthologies such as *Make Shift, Ride the Star Wind, Sharp and Sugar Tooth, Deep Signal,* and *Battling in All Her Finery.* Select stories can be read in German, Spanish, Vietnamese, Estonian, French and Japanese translation.

Stories That Stick in the Brain:
A Conversation with Donna Scott

ARLEY SORG

Donna Scott was born in Dudley and is from the Black Country, an area in the West Midlands of England, "so-called for the rich coal seam running through the land . . . Although folks from one side of my family were salt hawkers, a semi-itinerant traveling clan, the irony is my DNA isn't very well traveled at all, and my 23andMe map is just one great blob exactly where I'm from." Scott earned a BA with honors in English and French from Keele University, with subsidiaries in Spanish and energy studies. At Keele, she also earned a postgraduate certificate in education in French and German. Later, she earned an MA in English at the University of Wolverhampton. "I can see how recent government decisions have affected university course offerings, and my alma mater no longer offers any modern language course, which is such a shame. I went to an incredibly visionary university that had broad, interdisciplinary education at the core of its ethos."

Before launching the *Best of British Science Fiction* series, Donna Scott had a number of short fiction sales, including "Fool's Gold" in 2009 anthology *Under the Rose* (Norilana Books, edited by Dave Hutchinson); "Lord of the Lyceum" in anthology *The Bitten Word* and "Arthur The Witch" in anthology *Shoes, Ships and Cadavers: Tales from North Londonshire* (both published in 2010 by NewCon Press, edited by Ian Whates); "Hands" in 2013 anthology *Daughters of Icarus* (Pink Narcissus Press, edited by Josie Brown); and more. Her career in the publishing industry has included freelance proofreading and copyediting for Immanion Press, Rebellion, Games Workshop, Angry Robot, Oxford University Press, and Gollancz, as well as coediting at magazines *Focus* and *Visionary Tongue*. She also edited 2023 anthology *Dark Horses*, published by her own recently started publishing house, The Slab Press. She is a director and former chair of the British Science Fiction Association.

Donna Scott lives in Northampton, in a Victorian shoemaker's house, and works in learning and development for a private company. She has done many things besides publishing, including running a pub for a year and working as a teacher. She is also a comedian: "I'm part of a multi-award-winning children's comedy group called The Extraordinary Time-Travelling Adventures of Baron Munchausen, and I have more recently established a sketch duo with my husband called Prison Biscuit, which got to the quarterfinals of Sketch Off! last year."

Published in 2017 by NewCon and edited by Scott, *Best of British Science Fiction 2016* launched a new series "showcasing the talent of British and British-based science fiction authors." The seventh volume won the inaugural BSFA Award for Best Collection or Anthology. Publisher Ian Whates and editor Donna Scott have produced an edition every year, with the latest, *Best of British Science Fiction 2023*, due this month.

What were the works that you grew up reading? What were the things that you loved, that you feel have a lot to do with where you are now?

These days I have far too many books, but I can remember being at nursery and only having one: a storybook about a boy and girl who go to a funfair, and I drove my mom mad with it. We didn't have much money back then, but I had learned to read so quickly at the age of four that my mom had no choice but to sign me up for a library card.

As it was quite a small library, I reread a lot of favorites in there. I read all the Doctor Who books, and Rentaghost books, and novelizations of things I'd seen on screen like *ET*, *Ghostbusters*, and *Metal Mickey*. I read Rumer Godden's *The Dolls' House* over and over, all the *Oz* and *Heidi* books (those I borrowed from a friend), loads of Winnie-the-Pooh, Rupert Bear, and Enid Blyton. Then there was John Christopher, Alan Garner, Kenneth Grahame, Nina Bawden, Richard Adams, and I started with some of the lighter books by Helen Cresswell and Judy Blume, who I continued reading into my early teens. At that time, I also read Douglas Adams, the *Red Dwarf* books, Ellis Peters, Colin Dexter, Thomas Hardy, D. H. Lawrence, Terry Pratchett, Sue Townsend, and Dante. I was quite an eclectic reader, really. I still like to really mix up my reading, and though science fiction and fantasy take up most of my attention, I love contemporary books that are thoughtful and funny, and the odd crime thriller too.

There were some earlier "Best of British" genre books, but yours has stood the test of time better than most did. Do you see your anthology series as part of a lineage, or do you see it as very separate and perhaps different from what other editors did before?

I started out with some great "Best of British" stablemates at NewCon in Fantasy and Horror. I wish we still had those series too; they were wonderful! Jared Shurin and Johnny Mains were already well-known and successful editors, and their work has just taken them in a different direction, where they continue to achieve great things. At the moment I jokingly refer to Lavie Tidhar as "my great nemesis" because he is doing some wonderful things with *The Best of World SF*.

Can "British" SF rank alongside "World" SF? I think so. However, in recent years, we have heard our bullish politicians go on laughably about how "world-beating" British things are, and that irks me because it's a dog whistle to jingoists. But my series is not inward-facing nor parochially concerned. I don't think we could do it without a healthy global English-language short-fiction market, or a diversity of writers who just happen to be from or based in the UK and Ireland, and an interest in those diverse voices from the reading public. That said, I think the particularities of place and time can definitely influence art, and British stories have a certain flavor to them. We can be self-deprecating souls with a penchant for black humor.

As for my anthology series, I'm thrilled that it has found its fans. I never expected to be at the helm of a series with serious longevity. Alan Moore lent me his Judith Merril anthologies when I started, and I reckon she and Gardner Dozois are the giants whose shoulders we all stand on. My series is but a youngling compared to theirs.

How did this series start, what were you hoping to get out of it?

I was very kindly asked to edit this series by Ian Whates of NewCon Press. Ian started NewCon Press by publishing anthologies and has had a few guest editors over the years. A best-of series seemed a logical next step. Ian is a very kind friend, and I am motivated to do a great job for him because he's one of the best human beings I know. He works so hard and has done so much to help newer voices find their footing. We can't show him enough appreciation. He's a brilliant writer, editor, and publisher. I hope I've at least helped people discover NewCon Press and the other wonderful books that they do.

As someone who has scrutinized British short science fiction over nearly a decade for these books, have you identified changes in trends, things that remain the same, and things that are dramatically different since the first book?

I always include a little commentary on trends in my introduction. Real-world events are often mirrored in the stories I see coming through. When can't we say that times are turbulent or interesting? But over the past eight years, they have definitely been . . . well, awful. In Britain, at least. I think this has made for good science fiction. My series has coincided with a pettier, more argumentative Western political discourse, writ-large on the meniscus of the social media bubble, which looks nigh on set to burst on itself. I think we are all a little fretful about what we might do in a post-social media world, particularly as the nature of the Internet changes.

Some of the fretfulness has changed over the years: alienation and isolation were strong themes post-Brexit; reproductive rights loomed large in the Trump years. Then there were newly imagined diseases, and emotional robot stories increased during the Lockdown, as did terraforming and settling on new planets, possibly influenced by all the billionaires launching their rockets over that short space of time. Most recently the influence of AI has been felt, and mostly in a fearful way. Ecology and climate themes have been consistent over the years.

Do you feel that British science fiction is different from science fiction in the US, and perhaps from other places around the globe? How would you describe the relationship between British science fiction and works from other locales?

I have worked on an anthology of Chinese science fiction quite recently, and what stands out for me is how philosophical those stories are. There's not so much of that in British science fiction. US stories are very big on the actual storytelling, and there's lots of dialogue, but it does its job. I think the major differences between US and British science fiction reflect the sociohistorical gaps between us. We speak the same language, but "class" means something different to us, and the British are obsessed with it. We also have a slightly different attitude to capitalization generally. A real horror story for us would be a healthcare system that's not free at the point of use, and I've got some stories in mind that I've included that relate to this scenario.

Are there any stories, across the span of these anthologies, that still linger in your memory as more notable than most? And if so, what are they, and what is it about them that makes them stand out?

The first story I would recommend is "Assets" from *Best of British Science Fiction 2022* by Keith Brooke and Eric Brown, and the second would be their story from the previous year, "Me Two." I can well-imagine as collaborative writers they had to live in each other's heads a lot, and these two stories perfectly conjure up ideas of empathy and humanity—the earlier story in a sweet, sad way, and the later one making you wonder how that spark is missing from the protagonist. There sadly won't be any more of those stories, as Eric passed away last year, but I urge you to go and discover as much work by them as possible.

Other stories that stick in the brain include Matthew de Abaitua's "The Escape Hatch" because it's so very unusual and uncanny, with a WTF ending. I love Neil Williamson's "A Moment of Zugzwang" too, with its precise scene-setting and skillful use of vocabulary, Laura Mauro's "Looking for Laika," concerning the famous dog, and Ida Keogh's mouthwatering and romantic "Infinite Tea in the Demara Café." Val Nolan's "Cofiwch Aberystwyth" is beautifully written.

Are there venues or editors or even anthology series that you come back to again and again as reliable sources for some of the best stories in the industry?

There are writers who burst with so many great stories, you're almost always guaranteed to find something by them in each book: Lavie Tidhar, Liam Hogan, Robert Bagnall, Rhiannon A. Grist, Teika Marija Smits, and Fiona Moore to name just a few.

Are there any authors out there that you feel are underrated and deserve more attention than they get? And what works by them would you love for people to read?

Absolutely every single writer who has appeared, to be honest. Some people are just starting to get noticed; others are more established names but deserve yet more light. I would love to see more attention given to writers like David Gullen (*Shopocalypse*) and Susan Boulton (*Hand of Glory*). I don't want to miss people out, so I will just say again—everybody!

You are a writer—among many other things. Has working on these books had an impact on your own work?

Yes, I'm now very unlikely to start a story with lots of dialogue in an undescribed void, because I'm cheesed off with stories that start that way, even though rather a lot of them seem to get published. I think it has made me a more confident writer too, and I can write a short story much more quickly than I used to and make it more rounded. I know more about how to play with ambiguity, rather than just being ambiguous by mistake. What it hasn't given me is more time to write stories or do the admin of submitting stuff I've finished, more's the pity.

If readers were to look at one thing you wrote, what would you most like them to look at, and why?

I've a soft spot for "Siren's Song" in PS Publishing's *No More Heroes* anthology, which is a fantasy story about Chris Cornell, the singer from Audioslave and Soundgarden, and to some extent his friend Andrew Wood from Mother Love Bone. I immersed myself in the world of grunge writing it, and it gave me a fresh perspective on that music. Plus, it's just a beautiful book!

What do you see as the future of The Best of British Science Fiction series, what are your plans and hopes?

Keep going, of course!

I've also started up my own press called The Slab Press, and I'm working on an anthology of humorous science fiction, on which I'm making my decision right now, so of course in the future when this interview comes out, this will be oldish news.

I also have plans in the next year or so to try to move away from Northampton town center and all its temptations, so that a life of self-inflicted eremitism will result in more writing happening.

Is there anything else you'd like readers to know about you, this series, or your work in general?

I am bringing back my podcast *Champagne Social Butterflies* in late summer to talk to fellow creatives about how a multidisciplinary approach (nice way of saying "lack of focus") either helps or hinders them in their creative endeavors.

ABOUT THE AUTHOR

Arley Sorg is an associate agent at kt literary. He is a two-time World Fantasy Award Finalist and a two-time Locus Award Finalist for his work as co-Editor-in-Chief at *Fantasy Magazine*. Arley is also a SFWA Solstice Award Recipient, a Space Cowboy Award Recipient, and a finalist for two Ignyte Awards. Arley is senior editor at *Locus*, associate editor at both *Lightspeed* & *Nightmare*, a columnist for *The Magazine of Fantasy and Science Fiction* and an interviewer for *Clarkesworld*. He is a guest critiquer for the 2023 Odyssey Workshop, and is the week five instructor for the 2023 6-week Clarion West Workshop, among other teaching and speaking engagements.

Imperfectly Transparent:
Conversation with China Miéville

ARLEY SORG

China Miéville was born in Norwich and raised in Willesden; he grew up in London with his mother and sister. His mother was initially a waitress and then trained as a teacher. She wrote a book and translated from Italian and Spanish. Miéville worked in Egypt and Zimbabwe for a year before attending university at Cambridge in 1991. Early on he switched majors from English Literature to Social Anthropology, ultimately earning his BA in Social Anthropology at Clare College, Cambridge; and then his MSc and PhD in International Relations (the topic being international law, specifically jurisprudence) from the London School of Economics. He also held a Frank Knox Memorial Fellowship at Harvard University. "I taught Clarion, that one time. I was an Associate Professor of Creative Writing at the University of Warwick in the UK, for some years. But I've never actually *taken* any creative writing courses."

China Miéville has lived in Providence and Chicago but is currently based in Kilburn, London. "I am also increasingly spending extended periods in Berlin, a city that has become very important to me." He has been a full-time writer for over twenty years. He once worked as a full-time subeditor (similar to a copyeditor in the US) for *PC Dealer* magazine. "I was intending and expecting to be an academic—hence the PhD—but the fiction writing took off early in that process. I still published (and publish) scholarly work, when I can, but I live off writing, rather than academia."

Debut novel *King Rat* was first published by Macmillan in the UK in 1998, followed by *Perdido Street Station* in 2000, which launched the New Crobuzon series. *King Rat* received heaps of acclaim and landed on a number of awards lists, including a nomination for a Stoker Award; *Perdido Street Station* was a finalist for numerous awards and won the 2001 Arthur C. Clarke Award, a British Fantasy Award, and Ignotus and Imaginaire awards. Set in the same world, 2002 title *The Scar* won a British Fantasy Award, a Locus Award, and received a Philip K. Dick Award special citation, as well as numerous other nods and nominations.

To date, Miéville has eleven novels out, most recently 2012 title *Railsea* (Del Rey/Ballantine in the US, Tor in the UK) and 2016 title *The Last Days of New Paris* (Del Rey in the US, Picador in the UK); novella-length books such as 2016's *This Census-Taker* (Del Rey/Picador); two collections; and much more. He has been up for most of the major genre awards, multiple times, and won many of them, including Hugo, World Fantasy, BSFA, and Kitschies wins for 2009 novel *The City & The City*. To call him "accomplished" would be an understatement.

His latest is *The Book of Elsewhere*, coauthored with Keanu Reeves and due from Del Rey this month. The novel is "inspired by the world of the *BRZRKR* comic series Reeves created with writer Matt Kindt and artist Ron Garney, published by BOOM! Studios."

What is your usual process for writing novels, and how has your process changed over the years?

I don't know that I have a "usual" process, really—some books are extraordinarily difficult to write, some somewhat easier. One novel took me less than a year to write; another nineteen years, and it's not quite finished. Except in the broadest possible terms, I guess there are certain generalizations. I start with structure and outline, finesse that at some length, then go into the specifics. I know there are outstandingly brilliant novelists who abjure plotting in advance, but I absolutely can't do it. I tried once, and the book just meandered and went nowhere. And I felt unsafe the whole time.

What was "breaking in" like for you? Are there novels that you trunked, started but didn't finish, or finished but just couldn't sell?

I have many short stories and I think two longer things that I've started and not been able to make work and stalled out on at various stages. They await possible resurrection, but I suspect they'll stay dead at this point. The first novel I sold, *King Rat*, was in fact the first novel I'd finished. The process of getting it published was just like lots of the textbooks say it will be: I kept sending out the manuscript to agents when it was done (it took me a couple of years to write). Lots of agents said no—then one eventually said yes. They submitted it to publishers, one of whom ultimately said yes. Not a particularly scintillating story, I'm afraid. No unusual circumstances or insights—though a lot of luck, as with anyone who ever gets published.

We occasionally see book collaborations of different kinds involving people in entertainment with established writers—such as Janelle Monáe's recent SFF anthology The Memory Librarian—but we generally consider people like Monáe and Keanu Reeves as "beyond reach." How did this collaboration come about?

Keanu got in touch with me. He had this collaborative project in mind, and he had, it turns out, enjoyed reading my stuff over some years, so he contacted me to ask if I was interested in working together. I should say, I had had absolutely no idea he had read any of my books until that point (why would I, after all?), so I was very surprised to get his initial message. Also very flattered, of course!

What was the initial inspiration for The Book of Elsewhere, and how did the story change across conversations, edits, and production?

The foundational idea was his, of course. He had this character, B/ Unute, who he had created and about whom, with Matt Kindt and Ron Garney, he had worked on the *BRZRKR* comic book. He was interested in exploring that character—or a version thereof—in other media, specifically, here, long-form fiction. He had certain ideas about the core principles of this character—what was, if you like, "nonnegotiable." They were simple and few, and beyond that, however, he was incredibly open-minded and interested to see what ideas we could come up with.

It always seemed to me—and he agreed—that there was no point doing this unless one used the forms. That is, there are things you can do best with a novel, best with a comic, best with a movie, and so on. There was never any point doing this unless we could lean into the "novel-ness" and try to do things and do them in ways that the other media would struggle to do. So we spent a good amount of time initially coming up not just with overall narrative ideas, but with ways of telling that story, that we felt were particularly suited to long-form fiction. And of course, I also had to be reasonably certain I was a good person to do this: it would have been a bad idea to start by saying "Yes let's do this," then seeing if we could figure something out. Instead, it was more like "What do you think of these ideas? How about if we did this?" and seeing if this had legs.

Once we'd agreed that we did, narrowed that down, got an overview and a narrative shape, and started writing, then it was a question of checking in with each other and with our brilliant editor, Ben Greenberg. We'd evaluate everything we could: the pacing, the clarity, the mystery, the characterization, et cetera, to see if we were being faithful to what we wanted it to be. Making it not just a decent *BRZRKR* novel, but the best novel we could.

The words "epic" and "fantasy" have been used to describe this book, which also features "a US black-ops group." Do you have thoughts on how this novel might be described, or where it might fit in terms of genre or literary definitions?

Ultimately, those kinds of questions have to do with marketing, rather than the novel per se. I don't mean that in a sniffy way: those categories definitely have a role. But they are, very literally, not my job to worry about too much. I'd go further: if I were to worry about them, it might well pull against focusing on the novel's own quiddity. So, in answer to this question, I can certainly gesture vaguely and say, yes, military fantasy, mythic mystery, or what have you. But these really aren't questions that bother me overmuch.

You are known as a writer who shifts styles, topics, genres, and tones, while often giving readers interesting concepts and intelligent stories. Thinking on your body of work, what are the elements that you see as characteristic of your fiction?

Generally speaking, I think writers are rarely the best people to judge what is characteristic of their own stuff: it's often other people who can see this more clearly. In fact, I think the idea that writers can be presumed to have the best insight into their own work can be really deleterious. They *might*, but they might not, and while I have my own ideas, of course, about the stuff I do, it would be a mistake to assume that I'm right about it. Perhaps there are elements bespeaking elements of surrealism, an aesthetic of estrangement (and strangeness, which aren't always the same things), an interest in political and social hinterland, an enjoyment of and engagement with the textures of prose itself.

What really excites you about this story and the project as a whole?

I was excited by the idea of trying to do all the above while honoring the source material. I've said it before, but there's a certain freedom and pleasure you can get playing with someone else's toys that is distinct from those you can get playing with your own. It's an old observation that, in literature, constraints can be enabling. (This is the insight of the Oulipo movement, among others.) I've said before that operating according to certain generic norms can operate like that—a set of constraints that actually encourages inventiveness and creativity—which is what can make it a pulp iteration of a technique we might otherwise associate with avant-garde traditions. In this case, beyond the generic norms, there was also the "constraint"—and I use this in the sense of simultaneous unique enablement—of needing (and wanting) this book to be "a *BRZRKR* novel." But that doesn't mean taking for granted what that is. That's why I want this book to be, as well as everything else, a surprise. I want readers to be surprised that it fulfills that remit and/ but does so in ways that are unexpected.

What can you tell us about B—"the warrior who cannot be killed"— what is interesting about B and his plight?

I won't say much here, because the answers to that comprise the novel itself. I don't mean just in the sense of "spoilers" (though, sure!): I also mean, if I could satisfactorily and simply answer that, the novel would be redundant. It's presumably one of the tasks and unique qualities of fiction (and art in general) that it can ruminate on questions and provide answers in unique ways.

All of which said! I'll say that one of the things I appreciated a lot about B, in Keanu's thinking, is that he believes himself to fervently desire mortality, but *not* death. That I think is an interesting and important distinction, and something on which we touch. In addition, and complicating that, it's also the case that B—like, to be clear, all of us—has imperfect access to his own desires and wants. None of us straightforwardly know what we want, or want what we want, or don't want what we don't want, and so on. One of the most interesting, inescapable aspects of humanity—and of B—is that our selves are imperfectly transparent to us. This is endlessly fascinating to me, and that's reflected in this book, too.

Publicity for The Book of Elsewhere mentions plans for a live-action Netflix film as well as an anime series. Did considering these expansions and iterations have an impact on the way the story took shape?

Really not. One of the things that was a true joy about the way Keanu approached this project—and was not something that I took for granted—was that he was entirely open-minded and enthusiastic about letting each project be its own thing. This is partly why we refer to this book as "inspired by" the *BRZRKR* comic, rather than being a novelization of it. You don't have to have read the comic to read the book. Of course, if you do, there will be Easter eggs and references that might mean something to you, but it was very important to us that this is a standalone book. Not only that, but beyond those baseline definitional qualities of B, the "universe" of the book may not be exactly coterminous with that of the comic. And as to the movie and anime, I have no idea, but I'd imagine it may well be a similar approach. This to me is vastly more interesting and provocative than getting straightjacketed about "lore."

Is there anything else you'd like readers to know about The Book of Elsewhere?

Nothing not covered above, except of course that I hope people enjoy it.

Your fans are always eager to see your work. What do you have coming up or in the works that you can tell Clarkesworld readers about?

I have a very big novel that I've been writing for about nineteen years that is currently with the publishers. It won't be for a little while, but it is coming out, and I hope before too long. It is the thing I've been writing for the majority of my adult life.

ABOUT THE AUTHOR

Arley Sorg is an associate agent at kt literary. He is a two-time World Fantasy Award Finalist and a two-time Locus Award Finalist for his work as co-Editor-in-Chief at *Fantasy Magazine*. Arley is also a SFWA Solstice Award Recipient, a Space Cowboy Award Recipient, and a finalist for two Ignyte Awards. Arley is senior editor at *Locus*, associate editor at both *Lightspeed* & *Nightmare*, a columnist for *The Magazine of Fantasy and Science Fiction* and an interviewer for *Clarkesworld*. He is a guest critiquer for the 2023 Odyssey Workshop, and is the week five instructor for the 2023 6-week Clarion West Workshop, among other teaching and speaking engagements.

Editor's Desk:
Where Did the Dark One Go?
NEIL CLARKE

I've been holding off on writing this editorial largely because I wanted to have more data in hand. I know that sounds ominous, so let me start by saying I can see a path forward, which is an improvement over other points in this year.

It's no secret that the last couple of years have been challenging. Between "AI"-generated nonsense spamming the submissions pile, Amazon wiping out thousands of subscriptions in a single day, and a million other much smaller things, I've frequently found myself throwing my hands in the air and seriously reconsidering my career choices. It doesn't last long, but it's been happening more frequently than it should. I'm routinely saved by the positives I find in this work and the people I cross paths with in the process of doing it. Not just my team, but the authors, artists, translators, readers, and even sympathetic strangers who have no idea what we do, but have heard our woes.

Last night, I received a reminder of that support. I became the fourth editor since 1989 to win the Locus Award for Best Editor. If you aren't familiar with the award, it's run by *Locus Magazine*–a monthly genre publishing industry periodical–and voted on by both their subscribers and the public. Previous winners include Gardner Dozois (17), Ellen Datlow (17), and David G. Hartwell (1). It's somewhat humbling to be in their company and for it to happen this year is particularly meaningful. Thank you to everyone that voted. It's nice to know that the work we're doing here is appreciated. It helps more than you probably know.

Much as I'd like to bask in that moment, our problems are still at the door and we don't have the luxury of waiting until the last minute to bring you up to speed. Last year, I said this about entering the Kindle Unlimited program for magazines:

...I can say that our earnings for the first year will be substantially below what we had been receiving. Critically lower, but it does lower the number of new and recovered subscriptions we'll need to acquire, so we're going to give it a chance. At worst, it buys time, but we are also very aware that we are playing with the dog that just bit us. We're proceeding with caution.

At this point, I can say that if we didn't take them up on their offer, we would have closed sometime in the last year. By holding our nose and working with them, we gained the time we needed to make substantial progress on rebuilding our subscription numbers. We've done better than I expected and not as well as I had hoped, but there is light.

Over the last few months, we've been in discussions with Amazon. It was promising enough that we agreed to a three-month extension for a painfully smaller amount (which they have not yet paid us). The offered contract for July forward was for an even smaller amount–a tiny fraction of what we once earned from them and well-below the rates we are paid for a similar number of subscribers anywhere else–but we were talking and making progress. Those talks, however, seized-up as new requirements entered the picture. Barring a miracle, we won't be in the program effective July 1st and, once again, we won't be able to inform those readers why. There's always a slim chance we get back in, but it's no longer something we can count on.

It's unlikely that the amount we would have received from continued participation would have been sufficient to close the gap, but it would have helped. Ironically, the same number of subscribers anywhere else, would close it and even provide a small margin of safety. This is not a completely unexpected turn of events. In fact, a few months ago, I referred to a darker editorial that didn't run. We've utilized the intervening time well, however, and that editorial is now committed to the dustbin.

That said, we are not quite out of the woods. Last month's editorial focused on marketing–a role we are still trying to fill–was the result of a careful examination of what we've been able to achieve over the last year and some of the patterns within our field. We still see it as a viable path forward. **We need approximately three hundred and fifty new subscribers** to return to the levels we were at when this mess started. That's the baseline for operating as we have been, which is still well-below the budget required to pay our staff a fair wage.

But wait, the Amazon money is gone and you're still below that!

Fortunately, there was an overlap between the two subscription programs and we set aside that surplus (and our rainy day fund) for this eventuality. That's going to cover the gap for several months and each new subscription we pick up in the interim extends it a bit further. All is not lost and we're far from ready to give up. Exhausted, yes, but still standing and a little more optimistic thanks to all of you.

Last year, I asked for your patience as we ramped up our quest for Amazon subscription independence. I'm just asking for a little more time, and if you're willing, a little more help. Spread the word and the word for today is "Subscribe."

ABOUT THE AUTHOR

Neil Clarke is the editor of *Clarkesworld Magazine, Forever Magazine,* and several anthologies, including the Best Science Fiction of the Year series. He is a twelve-time finalist and two-time winner of the Hugo Award for Best Editor (Short Form), the 2024 winner of the Locus Award for Best Editor, a four-time winner of the Chesley Award for Best Art Director, and a recipient of the Kate Wilhelm Solstice Award. His next anthology, *Best Science Fiction of the Year: Volume 8,* will be published later this year by Night Shade Books. He currently lives in NJ with his wife and two sons.

Robot in a flower field 02

COVER ART BY **NINJA JO**

ABOUT THE ARTIST

Ninja Jo is a freelance artist born in Ukraine. She has over two decades of experience in the traditional arts—such as watercolor, ink and oil—and over a decade as a digital artist. The subjects of her paintings are usually robots, science fictional, dark, and/or cyberpunk. Before becoming a professional artist, she worked as a photographer. Photography remains her second favorite thing after painting.

Made in United States
Troutdale, OR
08/01/2024

21692138R00087